Leonard MacNally

Fashionable Levities

A comedy. In five acts.

Leonard MacNally

Fashionable Levities
A comedy. In five acts.

ISBN/EAN: 9783337427016

Printed in Europe, USA, Canada, Australia, Japan

Cover: Foto ©Andreas Hilbeck / pixelio.de

More available books at **www.hansebooks.com**

Fashionable Levities,

A

COMEDY.

IN FIVE ACTS.

By LEONARD MACNALLY, Esq.

SECOND EDITION.

———

LONDON:

Printed for G. G. J. and J. ROBINSON
PATER-NOSTER-ROW. 1785.

TO THE

RIGHT HONOURABLE,

The Countess of SALISBURY.

MY LADY,

THE Attention with which you have
protected the British Stage, claims
the Gratitude of every Dramatic Writer:
I therefore take the Liberty of dedicating
this Comedy to your Ladyship, and humbly entreat your Forgiveness for not pre-
viously soliciting your Permission.

I have the Honour to be,

MY LADY,

With the greatest Respect,

Your Ladyship's most obedient

And most humble Servant,

LEONARD MAC NALLY.

Temple April 29, 1785.

On seeing Miss YOUNGE in the Character of Lady FLIPPANT SAVAGE.

THE two scenic Muses had long kept a distance,
 And scorn'd of each other to borrow assistance;
THALIA was pert, and MELPOMENE proud,
And though of admirers they both had a croud;
Not two rival beauties on earth could be seen
More tortur'd with jealousy, envy and spleen:
Till JOVE, to whom all the celestials submit,
In matters of WEIGHT, or in matters of WIT,
Interpos'd his command, saying, henceforth agree,
United in friendship as Sisters should be;
And grant, as a pledge that your union's sincere,
Your mutual pow'rs to some favourite fair;
If one can be found amongst mortals below
Deserving the attributes you can bestow.
The Sisters obey'd; but unfix'd was their choice,
Till MINERVA appearing with soul-moving voice:
While in scales of suspense both their fancies were hung,
Appeal'd to their senses, and pointed to YOUNGE.
To YOUNGE, where the *smile-stealing comic* we find,
With the *soft*, the *sublime*, and the *graceful* combin'd.
To YOUNGE who can each diff'rent passion impart, ⎞
Who *pleases* the *judgement*, but *conquers* the *heart*, ⎬
And *guided* by NATURE, is *followed* by ART. ⎠

PROLOGUE

To FASHIONABLE LEVITIES.

Written by Mr. CHALMERS.

Spoken by Mr. WROUGHTON.

IN Shakefpeare's days we only play'd the fool,
And men of fafhion gave—not took—the rule ;
Then Lords were grave, and ladies grave ftill,
And only *we*, and clowns had wit at will ;
His mind rejected former claffic lore,
And drew from Nature's never-ending ftore.
But authors *now*—we often prove the fact,
Muft fafhion court, to teach us how to act.
Expofe the follies whieh our ftatutes fpare,
And unprotected Virtue make their care.
All nature *now* is *cuftom* ;—*cuftom, law* ;
And here we bring—not what we *think*,—but faw.
Tis hard to vary your dramatic mirth,
When every folly gives it likenefs birth.
Which though, in life, your laugh they may command,
Will rather pall, than pleafe, at fecond hand.
'Tis harder ftill to fuit the general mind,
And all our audience in our int'réft bind.
Honeft John Bull, vex'd with the cares of life,
With heavy taxes and a fcolding wife,
Wifhes fome hours in hearing us to wafte,
And *galloping dreary Dun* is quite his tafte.—
Sir Foppling too, his brains with claret addle,
Pronounces *Comedy* to be a *Twaddle* !
His Lordfhip by the privilege of folly,
Is neither mufical nor melancholy ;
Thinks every honeft bard *a queer old Put*,—
" Damme ! there's nothing in a play like *fmut* !
The politician's all-commanding pate,
Wouid have us dramatize th' affairs of ftate :
Make whigs and tories fight, here face to face,
And teach the patriots, *Unity of Place*.—
Some cry for fentiment, and fome for wit,
And yet our claim to either won't admit.—
The Critic Bench !* for which there's no appeal,
Since for the town they judge, and act, and feel.
Did you but know what pangs an author fhares,
How throbs his heart with anxious doubts and cares !
Let paft indulgence your attention keep :
Though we be dull—*Juftice* fhould never *fleep*.
And if to-night no merit we can claim,
The want of *power*, not *will*, deferves the blame !

> * *Looking into the Pit.*

DRAMATIS PERSONÆ.

MEN.

Welford,	Mr. Lewis
Sir Buzzard Savage,	Mr. Quick
Capt. Douglas,	Mr. Wroughton
Cheaterly,	Mr. Farren
Colonel Staff,	Mr. Wewitzer
Nicholas,	Mr. Edwin

AND

Mr. Ordeal,	Mr. Henderson

WOMEN.

Widow Volatile,	Mrs. Bates
Clara,	Mrs. Martyr
Constance,	Mrs. T. Kennedy
Mrs. Muslin,	Miss Platt
Grace,	Mrs. Wilson
Honour,	Mrs. Webb

AND

Lady Flippant Savage,	Miss Younge.

SCENE, BATH: Time, One Day.

₊ *Those lines which are within inverted commas, are omitted by the performers in the representation.*

Fashionable Levities.

A C T. I.

SCENE, *Lady Flippant Savage's*
Dreſſing-Room.

Enter GRACE *and Mrs.* MUSLIN.

Mrs. Muſ. AND do you really prefer London to Bath, Mrs. Grace ?

race Why, I do ; in London there's ſuch
a noiſe—ſuch rattling of carts, waggons, coaches,
chariots and vis-a-vis ; then at night its ſo charming to ſee the flambeaux flying about from
houſe to houſe, like blazing ſtars !—But what
have you got there for my lady, Mrs. Muſlin ?

Muſ. A few cards of laces.

Grace. Foreign, I hope—we hate every thing
Engliſh, and wear nothing but foreign manu-
factures. *(Bell rings)* My lady's bell.——Any
new company come down ?

B

Mrs. Muſ.

Mrs. Muf. Have heard of none, except the wife and daughter of big Mr. Minikin, the great pin-maker from Threadneedle-ftreet. *(Bell rings.)*

Grace. Coming, my lady *(goes to a door in the back fcene.)* It is only Mrs. Muflin, my lady.

Lady Flip. within. I'll be with her immediately.

Grace. Let me have a few words with you before you go——Sir Buzzard and my lady had fuch tifting yefterday, you never heard the like—— They hate each other moft affectionately, that is the truth of it——

Enter Lady FLIPPANT SAVAGE *through a door in the back fcene.*

Lady Flip. So Muflin, *(fits)* Heigh ho! I'm all langour and laffitude!—Never knew Bath fo dull—Scarce any perfon of fafhion—Nobody one knows—This patch has a pretty effect— And you may go, Grace; and do you hear, Grace, let Mifs Conftance know I fhall be ready to go out in half an hour.

Grace. Yes, my lady. ⸤*Exit.*

Lady Flip. Muflin, take a chair;—this is certainly Englifh rouge, a vulgar natural red.— Did you fee my brute as you came in, Muflin?

Mrs. Muf. Saw two of them, dear pretty animals, in the hall, my lady; the little French dog was playing with the Spanifh monkey.

Lady Flip. Muflin, are you mad!—my dog and monkey brutes! fweet creatures! I was enquiring after the brute my hufband.

Muf.

Mrs. Muf. I afk your ladyfhip's pardon; I faw Sir Buzzard with Colonel Staff, and Mr. Cheaterly in the great parlour.—But I have fomething to mention to your ladyfhip—here are the laces—*(opening the box)* but it is not about the laces I want to fpeak—but——

Lady Flip. But what ?—Heigh ho ! hand me the Olympian dew—Muflin, I faw a charming fellow at the play laft night; and he faw me—Lady Holden certainly pencils her eye-brows—But the charming fellow, he took up my whole attention from the performance——I flatter myfelf I engaged his—his eyes were never off me—was dreffed in a new Parifian frock. ——Hand me the volatile falts, Muflin.

Mrs. Muf. My lodger, I proteft !—pick'd the pinion of a chicken at my humble table, laft night, and never ceafed talking of your ladyfhip.

Lady Flip. Hand me the rofe water—he fpoke of me, you fay ?—

Mrs. Muf. Heav'ns, faid he, what an air !—what grace ! then run on in praife of your lady-fhip's perfon and beauty; but when he heard your ladyfhip was married, poor youth, how piteoufly he figh'd.

Lady Flip. Good natured charitable foul !—but his name—who is he ?—what is he ? whence came he?—and who are his relations, Muf-lin ?

Mrs. Muf. Cannot anfwer one of your ladyfhip's queftions, except that his name is Welford; he came to my houfe yefterday, and talks of leaving Bath to-morrow morning.

Enter

Enter G R A C E.

Grace. Mr. Cheaterly requeſts permiſſion to wait upon your ladyſhip.

Lady Flip. Shew him up.   [*Exit.* Grace. Come to demand his winnings ;—loſt two hundred laſt night, could think of no card but the knave of hearts I ſaw at the Theatre.

Mrs. Muſ. The knave—the king of hearts your ladyſhip means ; and let me tell you a trump— never ſaw finer eyes ; then he has the leg of a ſoldier, and the hand of a lady——but is he to have the honor of——

Lady Flip. Of what ?

Mrs. Muſ. He ſays he has ſomething of a ſerious nature to communicate to your ladyſhip.

Lady Flip. Perhaps letters from ſome of my friends in Paris.

Muſ. Saw a large bundle of letters on his table.

Lady Flip. Then, Muſlin, I leave his introduction to you—ſhall be at home all the morning.

Muſ. Your ladyſhip's moſt obedient—I leave the laces. *(going)* Never ſaw a handſomer gentleman.   [*Exit.*

Lady Flip. What a giddy creature am I ? but a body muſt kill time—then the fellow is ſo elegant, *(riſes)* and Sir Buzzard ſo peeviſh ! ——the fatigue and apprehenſion which body and mind ſuffer after an unluckly run, are inſupportable ; my nerves are quite out of tune, but Muſlin has in ſome degree elevated my ſpirits.

Enter

Enter CHEATERLY.

Cheat. I condole with your ladyſhip on your hard run laſt night; the aces conſpired againſt you;—Renounce brag, the cunning of the game lies, not in—judgment of mind, but in command of muſcles.

La. Flip. To which I impute your uninterrupted ſeries of good luck.

Cheat. I am unfit for brag;—the warmth of my heart, particularly in your ladyſhip's preſence, *(bows low.)* keeps my features in continual rebellion,—but no perſon with a flexible countenance ſhould touch brag, the impenetrable looks of lady Frigid Midnight, have eſtabliſhed her an adept at the game.

La. Flip. And her nimble fingers give her command of the cards; but ſhe loſt temper when I got the black knaves; it was when you ſtood on my right, and lord Lackacre on my left hand.—" I have got the black knaves," ſaid I, " Lady Frigid"—" I ſee you have," ſaid ſhe, pointing to you and my lord,—then, as ſhe puckered up her mouth in an affected ſmile, down fell a few flakes of paint, and her ſkin appeared under the fractures, like *old* brick work peeping through the *new* invented compoſition.

Cheat. Her countenance was once tolerable, but a long run of ill luck, has ſtamp'd that irriſible diſcordancy, of hill and dale, which marks her viſage, and prevents the ſmiles of fortune, joy, or good humour, from unbending her to a laugh, or the ſmalleſt ſemblage of the amiable. *(Hums a tune.)* There is a ſmall matter between us, for which I have a very preſſing occaſion.

B 3   *Lady*

Lady Flip. (*Afide.*) I expected this! Ha! ha! ha! I cannot but laugh at your description of Lady Frigid.

Cheat. For heav'n's fake fay no more of her;—but, let me have the money. (*bows.*)

Lady Flip. The money! Pfha! You muſt have patience.

Cheat. Patience for a debt of honour!

Lady Flip. I have bills to pay—my mercer, milliner, and mantua-maker, are to be with me to-morrow, and people of that claſs, you know, are rude and importunate.

Cheat. But fuppoſe I point out a mode of diſcharging this debt of honour without diminiſhing your ladyſhip's purſe—what ſay you?

Lady Flip. If you have any thing to propoſe I can honourably receive, ſpeak out.

Cheat. Your ladyſhip is not uſually ſlow of apprehenſion;—it is true, I have not made an open declaration of my paſſion.

Lady Flip. Sir!

Cheat. But my eyes, my looks, have ſpoke the workings of my ſoul.

Lady Flip. (*Goes from him confuſed*) This I never fuſpected. *Afide.*)

Cheat. May I hope for your aſſiſtance towards my happineſs; I have long loved, doated, and deſpaired.

Lady Flip. Long loved and doated! I'm not furprized at that. (*Afide.*)

Cheat. Sir Buzzard knows of, and approves my paſſion.

La. Flip. Sir Buzzard approves it!

Cheat. He does,—and I cannot live——

Lady Flip. Hold, Sir! *(Aside.)* I'm aftonifh'd.

Cheat. I cannot live without her.

Lady Flip. Without her! without whom?

Cheat. Who but Conftance!—divine Conftance!

Lady Flip. *(Aside.)* Though I defpife the fellow!—I—I—but why fhould I be ruffled?

Cheat. She thought I was making love to herfelf. *(Aside.)*

Lady Flip. And wou'd you have me accefſary to the ruin of a young creature?

Cheat. There is no ruin intended;—I have open'd my mind to the lady,—Sir Buzzard is my friend, and I only folicit your intereft; I would marry Conftance.

Lady Flip. No ruin intended! could a greater curfe befal a young creature than to marry you! —who are you, Sir?

Cheat. Who am I, madam! a gentleman.

Lady Flip. I don't mean to afperfe your birth, Sir; but is not your ruling paffion play; your principal dependance cards and dice; your moft intimate connections jockies, grooms, gamecocks, and race-horfes? I am furprized you could look up to her.

Cheat. My fortune and family entitle me to look up to any woman.

Lady Flip. Then it muft be merely to look up; you are, no doubt, one of Fortune's favourites, and her favours follow you;—you have large eftates in expectancy, and confiderable rents in Bath, Wells, Scarborough, Southampton and Margate; nay, more, you have as many agents as the firft landed gentleman in the country.

Cheat. I don't underftand this treatment.

La. Flip. Your connexions, manners and con-

verfation

verfation would be perfectly agreeable to Conftance's turn of mind ;—her refpect for religion,
her morality, philofophy, and knowledge of
the belles lettres, would exactly coincide with
your ftudies in the arts and fciences of play.

Cheat. Arts and fciences of play—

La. Flip. I infinuate nothing injurious to your
profeffion ; the tefpect which profeffors of play
receive in preference to all other profeffors proves
it a profeffion the moft liberal, as well as moft
profitable. *(ironically.)*

Cheat. She will never forgive the infult of
preferring another woman to herfelf ; *(Afide.)*
Your tradefmen's bills, madam, are unpaid, your
ladyfhip's mercer and milliner—and people of
that clafs are fo importunate and rude ;—I do
not folicit you to take an active part in my fa-
vour, only promife not to be an enemy, and
the debt of honour is cancelled.

Lady Flip. You fay the debt of honour fhall
be cancelled. Are you aware that Conftance
has beftowed her favours on young De Courcy,
of York.

Cheat. Yes ; and that his paffion for play was
cooled at the laft York races, which obliged
him to take a trip to France for the recovery
of his finances.

Lady Flip. And his loffes fhe imputes to a con-
fpiracy between you and thofe friends of yours,
who were the oftenfible winners, and to whom
you introduced him ;—I fear you have no
chance.

Cheat. Chance !—leave me to that ;—I have
often won with the odds againft me ; then fhe
is a beggar, but my paffion is difinterefted.

Lady Flip. And pray now, how much of the
uncle

uncle's debt of honour is to be paid by this parental kindness to the niece?—I see into the scheme,—and here comes the unfortunate sacrifice.

Enter CONSTANCE.

Con. I underſtand your ladyſhip deſired to ſpeak with me.

Lady Flip. To inform you, my dear, of ſome engagements, but particular buſineſs calls me away for a few minutes, ſo I leave you to entertain Mr. Cheaterly. [*Exit* Lady Flippant.

Cheat. (*Aſide.*) Her modeſt bluſh puts even my impudence out of countenance!—your ſolicitude, madam, to avoid me, ſo ſtrongly indicates apathy to my addreſſes, I almoſt dread the poſſibility of convincing you I am ſincere; —do not turn from me in ſcorn; I may have ſome claim upon your gratitude, though no intereſt in your heart.

Con. Gratitude! Oh! Your abſence, Sir, I muſt inſiſt on; I will not, in future, be perſecuted by your preſumption!

Cheat. I acknowledge my weakneſs in purſuing the impulſe of my paſſion; reaſon checks me, but ſuch is the imperious violence of my affection, that even your ſcorn increaſes my deſires, by making you lovely in the midſt of anger, and the bleſſing I ſigh for, appears ſtill more valuable, more worthy purſuit, from the diſtant proſpect you give me of the poſſeſſion.

Con. Proſpect, Sir!

Cheat. Yes, madam, proſpect.

Con. You will be pleaſed, Sir, to withdraw—
[*walks diſconcerted.*
you are inſolent.

Cheat.

Cheat. Infolent! a hard word, madam, to a man who prefers you to every other woman,—— I may be bold, madam, but——

Con. I repeat it, you are infolent.

[*walks from him.*

Cheat. I am calm, madam; I know the impediment to my happinefs, young lady, and have fpirit to remove it.—Infolent! ha; you prefer a clandeftine correfpondence with a bank-rupt in fame and fortune, to the generous addreffes of a man, honoured with your uncle's approbation, and independent of the world.

Con. The engagements of my heart—but I will not weep—*(wiping her eyes)*—Sir——you have, with a bafe and mean cowardice, dared to traduce a generous, unfufpecting youth, whofe fortune you have affifted to ruin, but whofe ho-nour you can never taint;—a youth who, if prefent, you would not dare to look on with-out trembling. *(going.)*

Enter Sir BUZZARD SAVAGE.

Sir Buz. What's the matter now?

Con. Enquire of that gentleman, Sir.

Sir Buz. What a life I lead! my mind kept in a continual fever, you and your aunt are a per-petual ague to me;—her hot fits of levity, and your cool fits of prudery, operate alternately, and I am tortured by you from morning till night.

Con. I muft tell you, Sir, that fince your houfe cannot afford me protection, I fhall leave it; and, though deftitute of fortune, I know where to apply for an afylum. [*Ex.* Conftance.

Sir Buz. " I know where to apply for an afy-lum!"—She cannot have a knowledge of our fecret, or I would fuppofe fhe meant the Chan-cery;

cery; a man muſt now pay as much attention to his ward, as if ſhe was his child.

Cheat. True, and what adds to the grievance, if a young fellow marries an heireſs, he is obliged to ſettle her fortune on herſelf, though, per-haps, her perſon was a ſecondary object,—I ſhall never ſucceed here, Sir Buzzard.

Sir Buz. Piſh, why not ſucceed; a hundred to one but all ſhe has ſaid is pretence,—you know nothing of women's ſubtilty; they ſmile, they frown, they laugh, they weep, they l. ve but to deceive us, and lay a ſnare in every ar-ticle of their dreſs.

Cheat. De Courcy is the object of her choice.

Sir Buz. Why afraid of De Courcy? his friends at York races plucked the poor devil of a pigeon ſo bare, they ſcarcely left him fea-thers to fly into France.

Cheat. I was preſent;—may I depend on your aſſiſtance?

Sir Buz. Is not our bargain concluded?—on the day of your marriage with my niece, you return me my mortgages, the bill of ſale upon my horſes, and an acquittance of all de-mands.

Cheat. Depend upon it—I have pledg'd my honour;— aſſiſt me, and I will purſue my game, though ſhe keeps me at bay every ſtep.

Sir Buz. Cheaterly, I muſt look about me; I came down here for the recovery of my health, and am ſuffering under a precipitate conſump-tion of my purſe. Do you think the young clergyman plays fair?

Cheat. You mean parſon Spruce; could you ſuſpect a divine?

Sir Buz. Why, yes; I do ſuſpect your di-
vines

vines in their own hair, and boots, many of them I believe have thrown off morality with their wigs, and kicked away religion with their shoes.

Cheat. But Dr. Spruce has three hundred a year in the church———he won a cool fifty from me.

Sir Buz. A fifty ! I loft more to him than would purchafe four years of his income.

Cheat. Do you want cafh ? I can lend you a hundred ; here *(gives him a note)* with friends money fhould be a common commodity.

Sir Buz. Why I loft this note to Parfon Spruce laft night—he gave me a fifty and took it.

Cheat. Aye, Oh, I had it from him, he gave it to me for a bill on London.

Sir Buz. Here comes Colonel Staff and old Ordeal yoked together, very naturally, as two affes fhould be ;—I defpife them both : the Colonel never ferved abroad, yet he prates as bold as if he had experienced half a dozen foreign campaigns.

Cheat. And is poor and proud.

Sir Buz. Yes, but hopes to mend his fortune by marrying my fifter; I wifh him fuccefs, that they may mutually torment each other.

Cheat. Mark Ordeal, he is not a lefs extraordinary character than the Colonel, the fellow was a foundling, and never knew his parents, but having acquired a fortune by trade, impudently infults his betters, by preaching what he calls generofity.

Sir Buz. O, confound his generofity, he is always fetting a bad example with his charities,

relieving

relieving widows, providing for orphans, and portioning off young maidens; though ignorant as a Hottentot, he has got himself rank'd among the literati, and sets up for a philosopher —the fellow has come into life through as many shapes as an Orkney Barnacle, he was first a block, then a worm, and is now a goose.

Enter Colonel STAFF, *and Mr.* ORDEAL.

Col. Ha! ha! ha! I have been accusing Ordeal of avarice, and he denies the charge.

Ord. I do, avarice, though too often an attendant on age, is a vice foreign to my nature; no man can accuse me of accumulating money by unjust means, or of hoarding it when in my possession; whereas avarice is a dropsy of the mind—a disease that irritates and increases by the means used to assuage its thirst.

Col. Have you not refused to lend me a mere trifle, and being rich, is not that a proof of avarice.

Ord. Hear me;—I consider myself an agent, bound to answer for the distribution of that wealth with which heaven has bless'd my industry—the charge of avarice is more applicable to the spendthrift than the prudent, the spendthrift grasps at every man's property; yet no man is accounted avaricious who conforms to the custom of dissipation; though the spendthrift raises his rents, and starves his tenantry—borrows money and ruins his friend, or runs in debt, and makes bankrupts of his tradesmen, if he drives a carriage—keeps a train of servants, plays, drinks, and plunges into vice, the world will call him a damn'd generous fellow——I speak my mind —that's my way.

Sir

Sir Buz. Well, Colonel, how goes on your affair with my fantaftical fifter? She is a jilt, Colonel.—I hate a jilt.

Col. She will foòn furrender, I have got poffeffion of the counterfcarp, and fhall fhortly fet up the ftandard of matrimony upon the crown of the——

Sir Buz. Horn work—Eh?

Cheat. The widow has a confiderable fhare of the *toujours gai* in her compofition.

Sir Buz. Too much to promife conftancy; but then you old bachelors have fuch winning ways —but Colonel, keep a centinel on my fifter— time and poffeffion are two dangerous pioneers, the firft moulders the cement by degrees, and the other faps the foundation.

Cheat. Then the widow is fo frank, degagé and good natured, fhe may grant favors from charity and fenfibility, which other women would refufe from principle, or the prejudice of education.

Ord. What Mr. Cheaterly has advanced, contains profound gravity of judgment; but my Clary fhall have no modern education, I have engaged a maîter to teach her the Claffics, to manure the foil by cultivating the feeds of virtue;—yes, I will have Clary cultivated, for fhe is innocence itfelf: free from the bias of example, fhe is guided only by the impulfe of pure nature.

Cheat. A young lady could not have a more dangerous preceptor, the impulfe of pure nature will produce every evil that can arife from the politeft education.

Ord. I am convinc'd fhe is delicate as the er-
mine,

mine, which would die to preferve the fnowy whitenefs of its fur.

Col. Well faid, my old friend, amorous as May, though grey as December.

Ord. Grey! Nay, let me tell you, Colonel, though fnow has fallen upon the mountain, there is funfhine in the valley—Clara is an Aurora Borealis, a blaze in the regions of frigidity.

Sir Buz. Ordeal, ferioufly, now, are you going to marry this ward of your's for love?

Ord. Serioufly, I love the girl as I love my life; but if I did not, having no relations nor friends to whom I owe any obligation, I am determined to make her my heir.

Sir Buz. And no doubt fhe will bring you an heir in return, and then bury you.

Ord. Bury me! — Granted: when I fleep peaceable under the green turf, let her marry fome honeft young fellow, and their children fhall bear my name.

Cheat. A good way this to raife a family without trouble.

Ord. Family, I underftand your fneer, I was a foundling it is true, and cannot boaft anceftry; yet I have a heart fufceptible of the tender feelings and fweet folicitudes of humanity. Though I cannot claim relations of particular defcriptions, I know Adam and Eve were our primitive parents, therefore, confider the world one common family, and hold myfelf bound to all mankind by ties of fraternal love.

Sir Buz. And your family kindnefs is not confined to your brothers, but extends to your fifters too.

Ord. Clara's father was my friend, we ferv'd our apprenticefhip together, fet up in the fame

branch

branch of trade, he failed, and died poor, but I profpered—he was a worthy foul, and I never fpeak of him without tears. *(weeps.)*

Cheat. Ah! very good, Sir Buzzard; becaufe the father was his juvenile friend he would marry the daughter in his old age.

Sir Buz. A pretty excufe for a vicious ppetite.

Col. Hear, hear!

Ord. Clara's father, when on his death-bed, bequeathed her to me as a legacy, it was a bequeft of confidence, and I efteem it more than if it had been a million: he bequeathed her to me an infant without a mother, without relations, without friends, without fortune.—Now, though rich in the liberal gifts of nature, who hath endowed her with an exuberant hand, yet being poor in worldly. fubftance, fhe hath but few attractions for a hufband; the knight errants of thefe days are Argonauts—this is the golden age and every thing is bought and fold.

Sir Buz. Spoke in the true fpirit of commerce, my old merchant.

Ord. Let me tell you, Sir Knight, the fpirit of commerce is the beft fpirit in the nation; we merchants live by barter and fale it is true, but take this with you, fir, probity is our principle, and our character nice as a lady's.

Sir Buz. Here comes my moiety of mortality—here comes the origin of two thirds of my complaints, with my widow'd fifter, the Colonel's tormentor that is to be—fee, they fmile at fome mifchief in embryo—Ah, candied ginger, fugar on the outfide, fire within, fweet on the palate, biting on the tongue. Ordeal keep a

ftrict

ſtrict eye upon pure nature, the aloe is moſt
bitter when green. *(going.)*

Cheat. Nay, ſtay, Sir Buzzard.

Sir Buz. Stay, and my wife coming!—excuſe
me, I avoid her as I would an epidemic com-
plaint.   [*Exit.*

En: - Lady F L I P P A N T S A V A G E *and Widow*
V O L A T I L E.

Wid. Are you here, Colonel? I follow you
as the little bird does the cuckoo—Mr. Ordeal,
your moſt obedient, how is pretty Clara, and
when are we to call her Mrs. Ordeal.—You
rear her quite a domeſtic animal, ſhe is never
ſeen abroad.

Lady Flip. Nor at home, ſiſter, not even at
the windows.

Cheat. He fears the ſun would ſpoil her complexion.   ‧

Ord. She hath indeed a lovely complexion,
glowing and bright as the Tyrian dye, not a
modern local bluſh, that hides ſhame inſtead of
diſcovering it; but ruddy health moving in
varied tints—the lily and the roſe vying for
pre-eminence on her cheek!—O ſhe is pure nature!

Wid. But when introduced to life thoſe roſes
will blow, thoſe lilies will fade.

Ord. She ſhall never get into any life, but
where they may blow and fade naturally—her
real face ſhall never be concealed under a coun-
terfeit; ſome ladies coin complexions, and ſhould
be puniſhed for high treaſon in defacing beauty.

Cheat. Bravo, old Ordeal! bravo!

Ord. I reprobate impoſition of charms! a
reverend biſhop declared to me he was married

C   two

two years before he faw his wife's face, and that was by accident.

Lady Flip. I am aftonifhed a gentleman of your age can be fo fcandalous, fo malicious, but it is the nature of wafps to retain their buz after they have loft their fting.

Wid. Our gaiety provokes their fpleen; thefe ancient gentlemen rail at women for fpeaking fcandal, yet refort in groupes to every place of public entertainment, ogl'ng with their telefcope eyes to difcover blemifhes on beautiful objects —now here's a piece of antiquity !

(turning Ordeal round)

Ord. I have not pretended to juvenality fince the crow's feet appeared near my eyes; nay, don't bite your lips, widow, lines will appear in the fkin after thirty, and are the harbingers to wrinkles.

Enter a Servant.

Serv. The chocolate is ready, my lady.

[Exit. Serv.

Lady Flip. Sifter, let us in—Mr. Cheaterly—

Cheat. I attend your ladyfhip.

Ord. Can I pay my refpects to Conftance, my old friend's daughter ?

Lady Flip. You will probably find her in the ftudy—poor Conftance takes the humblenefs of her fituation too much to heart.

[Exit L. Flip. Cheat. and Wid.

Ord. Colonel, I knew the father of Conftance intimately, a ftout fellow and ferved his country long and well—he ferved abroad—

Col. Hem !

Ord. Strict honour was his principle—but alas, he experienced that was not the medium

to

to promotion—so finding carpet soldiers like you promoted over his head, he went to India.

Col. This widow of mine, Ordeal, hath a prolific flow of wit and spirits.

Ord. Yes, and egad I thought she struck you dumb—she has a prolific tongue too, sharp as the arrow of a Bornean Indian, and tipp'd with poison; your union with her will be happy— perfectly happy—though I recollect she compared you to a cuckoo, a bird of omen; yes, a cuckoo is a very ominous bird—pray, Colonel, is the widow skilled in augury?

Col. Damn your cuckoo! but your speaking of augury reminds me of a circumstance at the siege of Prague—a flock of rooks——

Ord. I must go pay my compliments to Constance.

Col. At the siege of Prague—when the Prussian grenadiers advanced *(holds Ordeal)*

Ord. Were you at the siege, Colonel?

Col. My regiment was there—I have served my country.

Ord. Oh, yes, you have done great service to your country—at home—by censuring those who have fought for her abroad.

[*Exit.*

End of the First Act.

A C T

A C T II.

S C E N E I. *A Chamber.*

Lady FLIPPANT *and* WELFORD, *seated.*

Lady Flip. SIR, I muſt ſay you preſume too far.

Wel. I ſaw your ladyſhip and admired, and if that be preſumption, who is free from it? admiration naturally produced a more tender emotion—I communicated my feelings to Mrs. Muſlin ;—Mrs. Muſlin reported them to your ladyſhip, and your ladyſhip, with a mind, liberal as your perſon is elegant, permits me to throw myſelf at your feet.

Lady Flip. You have miſconſtrued the liberty I allowed—my houſe is always open to perſons of faſhion, and as a viſitor only I expected you.
(riſes.)

Wel. Nay, madam, your privy counſellor informed me I ſhould be admitted into the interior cabinet, and your principal lady in waiting introduced me in form accordingly.

Lady

Lady Flip. And fhall I call her now, fir, to
fhew you the way back ? *(afide)* pleafant impudent fellow.

Wel. You are not fo cruel—I fee pardon
beaming from your eye, and frolic fmiling on
your cheek.

Lady Flip. " And fhould I pardon, from that
" inftant, the fervile fuppliant, now at my feet,
" would lofe all fenfe of obligation, and from the
" miftrefs's flave afpire to be her tyrant."

Wel. " I neither defire to be flave or tyrant,
" but to love upon equal terms—you confent—
" I read it in your eyes—and I am fecret as the
" grave."

Lady Flip. " Secret you may be, but it is not
" the mere colour of reputation can protect a
" woman's honor.—I might perhaps carry on an
" intrigue with fecrecy, but my mind"——

Wel. " Upon my foul I have no defign upon
" your ladyfhip's mind, my heart is captivated;
" and if I did not totally mifunderftand my good
" friend, and your ladyfhip's very good friend,
" Mrs. Muflin, a certain perfon, (whom modefty
" will not permit me to name) is not totally in-
" different in your opinion" *(bowing)*

Sir Buz. (within.) Grace, where is your
lady ?

Lady Flip. Sir Buzzard's voice !

Grace. (within) My lady, Sir !

Sir Buz. Yes, your lady, ma'am !——

Grace. (fpeaking very loud) She is in her own
room, fir, but I believe not yet drefs'd—I'll let
her know you want her, fir.

Enter

Enter G R A C E.

Grace. As I hope to be faved, here is my mafter, and in one of his gruff humours, quite in a tantrum—the gentleman cannot go out that way—follow me.

Lady Flip. Into the next room—make hafte
(*pufhing Welford.*

Wel. I go, perhaps into the interior cabinet—This alarm I truft will convince your ladyfhip that in love, as in war, delays are dangerous—Go on, Mrs. Grace.

[*Exeunt Welford and Grace.*

Enter Sir B U Z Z A R D. *(he fits)*

Sir Buz. What an infernal life I lead !

Lady Flip. What has rais'd the ftorm now ?

Sir Buz. Why afk !—you know I am married—and married to you—I am my own mafter, and hate impertinent queftions—I have loft my money—I am glad of it.—Oh ! I wifh I had never married

Lady Flip. (*fighs*) And I, with all my heart.

Sir Buz. Yet you leaped at my offer—you were glad to fnatch at me—

Lady Flip. Who I ? I was feduced into the match !—have I not brought reputation to your houfe, fir ?

Sir Buz. Reputation to my houfe !—you have turn'd my houfe topfy turvy, infide out ; you have irritated me into a complication of complaints, and reduced my fortune to galloping decay—have fretted me down to a mere fkeleton.

Lady Flip. Sir, fome refpect is due to my birth ;—I am daughter to a nobleman, and
till

till honoured with my hand, your family could
not boaſt a drop of blood in their veins.

Sir Buz. No blood in their veins! I, indeed
have loſt both fleſh and blood ; no blood in my
veins !—Have I not lent your brother money—
your uncle, money—your couſins money !—
which of your honourable, or right honourable
relations are out of my debt ?——If I had no
blood in my veins, how the devil have you and
yours bled me ſo plentifully ?

Lady Flip. I deſpiſe your meanneſs—

Sir Buz. Your family are leeches—I could
never ſhake them off.

Lady Flip. Sir, your connexion with me was
an honor, which with all your land and wealth,
you had no right to expeƈt. What was your
family before your union with me ?

Sir Buz. Men and women.

Lady Flip. Could they boaſt antiquity ?

Sir Buz. Yes, my grandfather lived to ninety
—my father to eighty-ſix.

Lady Flip. You married me——

Sir Buz. To perpetuate my family—are you
ſatisfied ?

Lady Flip. No, I am not ſatisfied.

Sir Buz. I know it, I know it.—I know it.

Lady Flip. " My anceſtors can be traced to
" the Normans—the Danes—the Saxons."

Sir Buz. " Which only proves you have ſprung
" from pirates and invaders ; but what is it to me
" if you were related to the Piƈts, the Scots, or
" the Romans ?—I am a Savage !"

Lady Flip. " Yes, you are a ſavage indeed—

Sir Buz. " And the Savages let me tell you,
are the oldeſt and pureſt blood in the country."

Lady

Lady Flip. (*aside*) How shall I get rid of him —Sir Buzzard, you don't intend to stay here I hope?

Sir Buz. You hope so, do you?—I am glad of that, then here I shall have a comfortable nap. (*sits down and composes himself*)

Lady Flip. (*aside*) I'll raise the spirit of contradiction to send him off (*draws a chair and sits by him*) now that is kind, thanks for your company, and I'll read, or sing a lullaby to compose you; shall I kiss you?—come now, smile my dear. (*takes off his hat*)

Sir Buz. I hate smiling, smiling is the cunning covering of deceit, (*rising*) and kissing ——am I in a habit of constitution for kissing?

Lady Flip. Am not I your wife?

Sir Buz. I feel you are—do not roll your basilisks—they have lost their fascinating powers.

Lady Flip. But you shall not go—

Sir Buz. Not go!—I am master of my own house!

Lady Flip. Then I will be mistress of my time;—I may find a companion.

Sir Buz. With all my heart—a woman who would keep her husband at home, is worse than a corn on his foot, there is no stirring at ease for her!—O that mine were cut off.

Lady Flip. You will go before me though, I shall wear weeds for my love—your face looks this instant pale as marble, and I can see " Here, lieth Sir Buzzard Savage," written on your forehead.

Sir Buz. I am ill it is true.

Lady

Lady Flip. Ill ! you have a mortal blackneſs under your eyes.

Sir Buz. Eh ! What !

Lady Flip. Do not ſtare ſo—it alarms me!

Sir Buz. My head ſwims !——I feel a palpitation here, juſt upon my temple.

Lady Flip. A dangerous ſymptom.

Sir Buz. I know it, and you are glad of it. Oh, Lord ! I ſhall preſently be enrolled on Death's liſt of Bath patients, who die where they come to live for the recovery of their health. 　　　　　　　　　　　　　　[*Exit.*

Lady Flip. Now to deliver my poor diſtreſſed ſwain from confinement. 　　　　　　　　[*Exit.*

S C E N E II. *Another Apartment.*

W E L F O R D *and* G R A C E *diſcovered.*

Wel. Nay, my nonpareil—my ſweeteſt, deareſt of all girls, you may believe every word I ſay.

Lady FLIPPANT *appears liſtning at a door in the ſcene.*

I have lov'd you——

Grace. Love me !—dear ſir !—Well, whether you ſpeak truth or no, I like to hear you ſay ſo—yet, I fear you are falſe-hearted, it was my lady you came to viſit.

Wel. Your lady ! no, no, child, you were the objeƈt, and I got myſelf introduced to the lady, that I might with more eaſe become intimate with the maid.

Grace. Cannot believe that—my lady is much handſomer than I—What a fine complexion !

Wel. Mere rouge !

　　　　　　　　　　　　　　　　　Grace.

Grace. White teeth !

Wel. For which she's obliged to the Dentist—

Grace. Charming hair !

Wel. All false.

Grace. Then, what polite conversation !

Wel. Psha, child she has not the native bloom of your cheeks, the nectarine of your lip, the pearl of your teeth, the natural curl of your tresses, nor the wit of your imagination.

Grace. (*aside*) How I likes to hear him praise me and abuse my lady !—and you really love me ?

Wel. Most devoutly—could we not retire to a more private chamber ? (*shews a purse.*)

Grace. Swear you'll not be false hearted.

Wel. By Jupiter, Venus, Cupid, and all the Gods and Goddesses, never (*shakes the purse*)

Grace. Then hear me swear (*lays her hand upon the purse*) by this purse (*takes it*) I like you.

Wel. Take it my girl—take it.

Grace. And by this ring, I'll (*lays her hand on his ring*)

Wel. My dear don't swear so often—but kiss me hussey—I have a secret to tell you.

Grace. " A secret ! but may not that secret " speak for itself hereafter, and discover all."

(*Lady Flippant comes forward.*)

Dear ma'am you can't think how the gentleman has been praising your ladyship's complexion, teeth, hair, and I don't know what.

Wel. Yes, I was praising your ladyship's—I —I—I—don't know what.

Lady Flip. There's no impediment now, sir, to your retiring, and I request you will instantly withdraw.

Wel.

Wel. For the prefent I fubmit to your rigid
and peremptory fentence ;—it is my way never
to deny or palliate my faults. When I travel
in purfuit of pleafure, I always take a view of
fuch beautiful feats as lie before me, and for the
life of me, l could not help cafting an eye of
this little fnug box, which lay fo convenient to
your ladyfhip's manfion-houfe. [*Ex.* Welford.

Grace. I hope your ladyfhip will excufe me;
—I thought I was doing no harm,—I thought
your ladyfhip difmiffed the gentleman, and your
ladyfhip knows we chambermaids have the fame
claim to our lady's caft lovers, as to their caft
cloaths.   [*Exit* Grace.

Lady Flip. Order chairs, and tell my fifter
I'll attend her to——Devil take the fellow,
yet I admire him for his impudence.   [*Exit.*

S C E N E   III.

Ordeal's Study.

Enter N I C H O L A S *and* D O U G L A S, *dif-
guifed in a fhabby Highland Drefs.*

Nich. And fo you were recommended by old
Corderius, the fchoolmafter, to teach our young
lady the Latin lingo.

Doug. Yes ; to inftruct her in the reediments
of the dead languages.

Nich. Dead languages! do you mean the
languages fpoken in the other world? for ecod
fhe can chatter glibby enough in the living
tongue.

Doug. I am to inftruct her, man, in Greek
and Latin.

Nich.

Nich. Greek and Latin ! will not that teach her ftrology and conjuration ?

Enter O R D E A L.

Here, Sir, is Mr. a—a—What's your name, Scotchey ?

Doug. Alexander M'Claffic.

Nich. He's Mr. M'Claffic, come from Mr. Corderius to learn Mifs Clary the dead languages, which he has got alive at his tongue's end.

Doug. Here, Sir, are my credentials.

(Gives a letter.

Ord. My friend Corderius gives you an ex·cellent character, young man, for honefty, and literary abilities, and you may begin with your pupil when you pleafe.

Nich. He has began with her already.

Ord. You are perfect mafter of the claffics, I prefume.

Doug. My father keept an academy, where I firft acquired the roodiments, and after I matriculated at Aberdeen; there I made an intimate acquantance with the philofophers, Chriftian, and Heathen,—the logicians, mathematicians, aftronomers, navigators, botanifts, chemifts, and aw the tribe of nateral philofophers.

Nich. What a number of fcholars are in Aberdeen !

Ord. Be filent, fool.

Doug. As to the claffics, I am maifter of Homer, Xenophon, Sophocles, Seneca, Virgil, Ovid, Terence, Salluft, Livy and Horace.

Nich. Have you learned all thofe gentlemen ?

Ord.

Ord. Silence, you inquifitive puppy.

Doug. I teach them aw, and will make the young lady miftrefs of them aw.

Nich. Miftrefs of them all ! Ecod fhe'll never remember half of her fervant's names ! but o' tag, rag, and bobtail; how comes it that with all thofe fcholars you've taught, you go fo poorly ? Ecod your cloaths are all in jeopardy. He ! he ! he !

Ord. Silence. Go you, firrah, and call mifs Clara.

Nich. I go—I go—I go—I go—I go—let me fee—he teaches muficians, magicians, and phyficians—and he'll teach her conjuration and ftar-gazing—and—mum. [*Exit* Nicholas.

Doug. You are, I prefume, Sir, a fcholar.

Ord. I never deny my ignorance—it is my misfortune, and a man fhould only be afhamed of his faults,—I do not underftand a word of any language but my native tongue, except a few phrafes I have picked up,—but I have read moft Englifh authors; born in poverty I was debarred the benefit of a liberal education,—I am candid—that's my way.

Doug. This is a common cafe.

Ord. No doubt one half of the literati are unlettered, and like light or Birmingham guineas, pafs for more than they are worth.

Doug. You intend to mary the lady yourfelf ?

Ord. Yes.

Doug. And you have fecluded her frae company, aw that was judicious—be cautious what men you introduce to her.

Ord. Yes; and women too,

Doug. That's right,—recreations which prudence

dence prohibits at home, and decency denies the exercife of in public, may eafily be enjoyed at the preevate houfe of a confidential friend.

Ord. You are right, there are many obliging, convenient, liberal-hearted, female beauty brokers, who fupport elegance and expence by trading in a contraband commerce of the fexes.

Enter CLARA *and* NICHOLAS.

Well, my girl,—your tutor has given you a leffon, I underftand.

Cla. Yes, Sir. *(Loud knocking).*

Ord. Who the devil is at the door?—I believe they have got a battering-ram, and are going to ftorm us after the manner of the Greeks and Romans. [*Exit* Nich.

Enter NICHOLAS.

Nich. Such filks, and ruftlings!

Ord. What's the matter?

Nich. There are cork rumps—hoops and high heels in the houfe.

Ord. Who knocks at the door?

Nich. They are covered with paint, patches and pomatum.

Ord. Who knock'd at the door?

Nich. Falfe hair, curls and perfumes!—don't blame me, they came upon me unawares; I pufh'd, and they pufh'd,—but they pufh'd harder, and overturned me.

Ord. Who overturned you?

Nich. They are full of flirtation, and giggling, and bedizened with gauze and ribbands; Lady Savage and her fifter, with their long tails fweeping behind.

Ord.

Ord. Lady Savage and her fister! Lady Devil and her imp !—Where are they?

Nich. Running all over the houfe—up ftairs and down ftairs, to and fro,—in and out—backwards and forwards—round about—here and there, and every where.

Ord. I am not at home,—there is no body at home—we are all out—I'll retire to my clofet; you will ftep with me, Mr. M'Claffic, and do you, my lamb, lock yourfelf up to avoid 'em.

[Exit Ordeal and Douglas.

Nich. He, he, he,—here is a blufter,—Ecod we fhall have rare fport.

Enter LADY FLIPPANT *and the* WIDOW.

Lady Flip. Where, my dear, in fuch hafte?

Cla. Indeed I cannot ftay—muft I not go, Nicholas?

Nich. Yes, you muft go,—go—go—go

[pufhing her out.

Wid. Be not alarmed, mifs, we are Mr. Ordeal's intimate friends.

Nich. Yes, mifs, they are our intimate friends.

Lady Flip. Come to vifit you, my dear.

Nich. Yes; they are come to vifit us,—my dear.

Wid. Where is Sir Ordeal?

Nich. Out—out—out (*Points to the clofet.*) (*Afide*) we fhall have fwinging fun.

Cla. Ladies, farewell. (*going.*)

Wid. Fie, my dear,—it would be impolite to leave company.

Nich. Mifs Clary,—Manners makes the man —we are teaching her the Latin lingo.

Wid. Are you very happy, my dear, on being on the verge of matrimony?

Nich.

Nich. Speak, my dear. (*Lady Flippant, and the Widow, stand on each side of Clara.*)

Cla. I cannot say I'm very happy ; nor I cannot say I am displeased ; I do not wish to be married, nor have I any objection to a husband——Heigho !

Lady Flip. But to confess the truth, you have no desire to marry Mr. Ordeal, he is such an old fellow ; though if addressed by a handsome, wealthy, good natured youth, you'd—Heigho !

Cla. Do not speak disrespectfully of my guardian—he is very kind to me.

Lady Flip. I approve your prudence in preferring an old lover to a young one ; after marriage you will no longer be confined like an infant ;— then you will enjoy such pleasure in making his money fly, and in seeing him approach the grave.

Wid. But for fear he should live too long, be sure you get him a physician.

Nich. A physician ! O, death !

Cla. My guardian has taught me how a married lady ought to conduct herself.

Wid. Let us hear, my dear pretty creature.

Cla. I have it by heart ; he has taught me, that all young men are cunning and deceitful, and that I must never listen to or believe their flattering tongues ; that a man and his wife are one person, and should act as if inspired by one soul !—that a wife should not complain of her husband to her most intimate friends, nor form any connexions without his approbation.

Nich. There's instruction for you ; you see we take care of her soul.

Cla. Moreover, he has taught me, that in private a wife should receive no company without

her

her hufband's knowledge, and in public fhould not think herfelf protected but by his prefence; that fhe fhould obey him in all things, and place her higheft delight in making him happy.

Lady Flip. Thefe were the duties of a wife in the laft century,---but we will inftruct you in the duties of a wife, who would cut a figure in the polite circles of the prefent day.---Sifter, begin.

Wid. Muft confider matrimony a means to increafe liberty, and defy fcandal.

Lady Flip. Muft retain your favourite ci-tifbeo, confidante, maid fervant and footman.

Nich. That will be, I.

Wid. See whom you pleafe, where you pleafe, and when you pleafe.

Cla. That muft be very pleafant!---go on.

Lady Flip. Muft be miftrefs of your own hours;---turn day into night, and night into day.——

Wid. Keep a feparate purfe, a feparate carriage, and a feparate bed.

Lady Flip. Never attend to œconomy, but fink, play, and fquander your money, to the laft fhilling, and ftretch your hufband's credit to the utmoft.

Nich. Here is work cut out for mantua-makers and milleners.

Wid. You muft always diffimulate in converfation with your hufband, and when you cannot deceive you muft infift---if he oppofes your will, rant, and laugh at him.

Nich. Ha, ha, ha!

Lady Flip. And if thefe fail, accufe him of cruelty, figh, fob, weep, fcream out, and fall into fits.

D   *Enter*

Enter ORDEAL *and* DOUGLAS.

Ord. I can contain no longer!---out of my
houfe!——

Lady Flip. Shame! Shame! What, liftening
to the private converfation of ladies?

Ord. Private converfation! open, abomina
ble inftruction,---how can you anfwer to your
confcience, for attempting to poifon a young
creature's morals!---retire, retire, my lamb.---

Cla. Farewell, ladies.

Wid. Adieu, pretty Clara.

Lady Flip. And remember our inftructions.

[*Exit* Clara.

Ord. Inftructions!——down-right libertine
principles!---you may laugh, ladies,---you may
laugh. Ha, ha, ha!

Lady Flip. }
Wid. } Ha, ha, ha!

Doug. Perhaps the ladies think their beauty
fufficient excufe for their levity,---but ah, they
are wrong---naething can atone for want of
delicacy, without which there can be nae charms
in the face, nae elegance in the perfon.

Enter Colonel STAFF.

Col. Ordeal, your moft obedient---call'd at
your ladyfhip's houfe, and Mifs Conftance inform'd me you were on a vifit here.

Wid. We came to fee Mr. Ordeal's pure nature, and he has affronted us!

Col. Affronted!---impoffible!

Doug. Haud your tongue, lady, haud your
tongue!---levity degrades a woman, however
her name may be elevated by birth, teetle, or
fortin.

Col.

Col. Who are you ?

Doug. A man.

Nich. Yes, and a fcholar ecod !

Ord (to the women) Out of my houfe !

Lady Flip. I'll prophecy for your comfort, if you marry Clara fhe'll foon draw a comparifon between your winter frown, and the fummer fmiles of a pretty fellow.

Ord. I defpife your prophecy---Oracles have long fince ceafed ; when they exifted the devil fpoke through them, which may be your lady-fhip's cafe.

Col. Ordeal, take care, I wear a fword.

Doug. I weer a fword.

Col. Do you daar echo my words ?

Doug. Do you daar echo my words ?

Nich. Knock out his teeth with one of your hard ones.

Col. Rafcal *(raifes his hand):*

Doug. Rafcal ! hear firft, and ftrike after,— you appear an officer, but I am convinced you are nae foldier ; touch but a hair o' my heed your hand, and the dee'l gáng away wi my foul gin I dinna fplit you through the crown.

Nich. Sir, Sir, fhall I bring him the old broad fword.

Col. There was juft fuch a fellow as this at the Havannah——

Ord. There were feveral fuch fellows at the Havannah, and fuch fellows only could have beaten the brave fellows who defended it,—were you there ?

Col. My regiment did fervice there—and if it had not been for a damn'd ague,—but no mat-ter,—I overlook this fellow's infolence,—but Mr. Ordeal, you have been too fevere on the ladies   D 2   *Doug.*

Doug. Too fevere on the ladies---I am your echo again---zounds, do you take the man for a Shrove-Tide cock, fet up to receive blows without returning them?

Wid. Let's go, we are not likely to receive protection from the Colonel.

Doug. I ken, madam, what you are.

Wid. Stand off, fellow——

Col. Thefe are ladies of honour.——

Doug. Their honour, like your courage, is in their own poffeffion, but remember the character of both is in the opinion of others.

Wid. Do you hear the fellow?

Col. He's mad, and not worth notice.

Lady Flip. Were I Clara, I fhould prefer a young Indian, though fure of being his widow, and burning with him in a month, to living with you for an age.

Col. Ordeal, you fhall anfwer this—but——

Doug. But what dare you fay?

Col. Say---I fay---my immediate duty is to attend the ladies.

[*Exit* Colonel, Lady Flippant *and* Widow.

Ord. My brave Caledonian! (*fhakes hands*) but here, here, ftep out and get yourfelf new rigged---(*gives Douglas money*).

Nich. Yes, he is out of feather and wants pluming.

Ord. But you, you firrah, if ever you let thofe women enter my doors again, out you go ---oh, what a fierce beaft, and a perilous enemy to the commonwealth, is a wicked woman.   *Exeunt.*

End of the SECOND ACT.

ACT III.

A C T III.

SCENE I.

Enter Lady FLIPPANT SAVAGE *and* GRACE.

Grace. SHALL I introduce the Gentleman, my lady?

Lady Flip. Yes,—no,—yes, Grace.

Grace. I like the gentleman, becaufe he likes your ladyfhip,—and that fhews him a man of tafte—I go.—*(going)*

Lady Flip. Stay, Grace,—let me ·confider, this interview may be attended with all the ill confequences of an illicit correfpondence.—what are you mufing on Grace?

Grace. I am thinking how very ugly Sir Buzzard is in comparifon with your ladyfhip's lover.——

Lady Flip. Sir Buzzard's plainnefs, Grace, is not his worft fault,—it is his peevifh afperity of difpofition renders him odious to me,—Grace, I will not fee this gentleman, it will endanger my reputation.——

Grace. Lay, my lady, but confider, *my* reputation, my *bonour* is pledged,— he is a delightful creature.—Then confider what an airy, nice dreffed gentleman he is—and confider, Sir Buzzard wears flannel under-waiftcoats, and fwanfkin ftockings.

Lady Flip. Can I ever again face Sir Buzzard?

Grace. If I was your ladyfhip, I would not face my lover too fuddenly,—no, I would re-

cline

cline upon the fopha,—(*fits*) loft in thinking,—
fo,—with my fan fhading my face thus, and
every thing about me. degagee.——

Lady Flip. You fay he waits.——

Grace. Or when the dear man approach'd,
turn fhort—ftrike him with the full flafh of my
charms, and fcream out. Ah!—(*fcreams and
ftarts up.*)

Lady Flip. Are you mad, girl?

Grace. A thoufand pardons, my lady, but
proteft I am befide myfelf.   *Exit. Grace.*

Lady Flip. There is no retracting, and I
think I *will* take him by furprife.—I'll keep
up the appearance of refentment, and have the
fatisfaction of hearing him humbly plead for
pardon.—(*fits, with her back to the door*)

Enter GRACE, *and* WELFORD *full dreffed.*

Grace. Now you muft acknowledge I am
your friend.

Wel. My fweet girl, I do acknowledge it—
                                        Exit. Grace.
A fine figure! (*taps lady Flippant on the fhoulder,
—fhe ftarts*) Madam——

Lady Flip. Heaven defend me!

Wel. Not from an ardent lover!——

Lady Flip. (*Afide*) I cannot fcold the fell at
he looks fo pleafant! — Pray, Sir, by wh
warrant do you come here?

Wel. I underftand from Mrs. Muflin, by
warrant from your own lips,—but the warrant
is incompleat till your ladyfhip has affix'd the
privy feal to it (*offers to kifs her*).

Lady

Lady Flip. A married woman can grant no-thing without the confent of her hufband.

Wel. Well thought on; but I do not come unprepared, man and wife are one perfon, and when a married lady gives me reafon to think a tete-a-tete would not be difagreeable, I always take care to bring my authority along with me.

Lady Flip. But fuppofe a lady fhould acknow-ledge your authority ;—your inclinations, I imagine, Sir, could not eafily be attach'd to a fingle object.

Wel. Yes they could,---though I candidly acknowledge I entertain an affection for the whole fex.

Lady Flip. Then there is an individual you prefer to the whole fex ?

Wel. There is.

Lady Flip. Handfome ?

Wel. Yes.

Lady Flip. Senfible ?

Wel. Yes.

Lady Flip. And you really prefer her——

Wel. If I denied it I fhould be infincere and unworthy your attention.

Lady Flip. And pray, Sir, may I enquire, who is the favourite fair ?

Wel. Nay, the lefs we fay, or think of her, the better, fhe is abfent——

Lady Flip. Yes, Sir,---I perceive fhe is abfent ---*(walks about)* and you too are abfent.

Wel. Yes, fhe is abfent,---and---Sir Buzzard is abfent, and we are together,- -and you are a fine woman,---and I am——

Lady Flip. What, Sir ?

Wel.

Wel. A man,---a young man, not a very ill made man, and a very well drefs'd man, with a brifk flow of fpirits, a warm heart, and a foul which at this inftant vibrates with fenfibility.

Sir Buzzard (within). I fay it is falfe, I left all the papers in London——

Lady Flip. I proteft Sir Buzzard is at the door ---you muft be concealed again——

Wel. Unfortunate! *(fhe pufhes him in)*

Lady Flip. You cannot get out of that room till I pleafe---*(fits)*

Enter Sir BUZZARD SAVAGE, and GRACE *walking lame.*

Grace. Oh, mercy, Sir, you have ruin'd me; oh, my lady, my lady, oh, oh, I fhall faint with pain; juft when I got to the door, there was my mafter, and not knowing it, I run plump againft him, and he trod upon my foot,---oh,--- but it is much better.

Sir Buz. *(fits)* A meffenger is come down from London for the title deeds of Profpect Farm,---do you know where they are?

Lady Flip. What fhould I know about your mufty parchments?

Sir Buz. Why not?---you fpend the rents faft enough---but I remember now, they are in a box that lies in the wardrobe in that room, and——

Grace. La, Sir,---I will get it.

Sir Buz. You are not tall enough to reach it.

Grace. But I can ftand on a chair, Sir, though I need not do that,---our new footman is in the clofet fettling your cloaths, Sir.---yes, Sir,--- our

our new footman, Sir, is in the clofet fett'ling your honour's wardrobe, and he'll help me.

Exit Grace.

Lady Flip. (afide) What can fhe mean? fhall I defire Grace to bring the box out to you?

Sir Buz. No, let the footman bring it out, I have not feen him yet,---Grace, bid the fellow bring in the box.

Grace (within) He's taking it down, Sir.

Sir Buz. Leave it in the clofet, I muft get fome other papers out of the fcrutore *(rifes).*

Enter GRACE *and* WELFORD *in a Livery, with a box.*

Grace. Come, young man, I'll get you my lady's cards for Wednefday's route, and they muft be delivered immediately.

Lady Flip. (afide) What a metamorphofis !--- you'll be expeditious.

Sir Buz. A good looking fellow ;---but ftand off ;---he is enough to fuffocate a man with perfume ! What's your name, Civet Cat?

Wel. (in a ftrong brogue) What's my name? I was chriften'd Patrick, your honour.

Sir Buz. An Irifhman !---eb,---heav'n knows we had blunders enough in the family before,--- *(looking on the box)*---this is the wrong box.

Exit Sir Buzzard into the clofet.

Grace. Yes, we have all got into the wrong box *(afide).*

Wel. When next we meet---*Exit.*

Grace. Nothing could be more lucky, my lady,---the new livery that came home for your laft footman George, lay in the bottom of my mafter's wardrobe. I muft fee him fafe out---

Exit.

Lady

Lady Flip. This is too mortifying, it hurts my pride—had I met a man of a generous dispofition—but here comes my torment, and reflection flies.

Enter Sir B u z z a r d *with* W e l f o r d's *Cloaths.*

Sir Buz. I have found more than I fought for, Lady Flippant;—who am I to thank for this addition to my wardrobe?

Lady Flip. Thefe cloaths!—you mean thefe cloaths!—he, he, he,—they are really very pretty cloaths---you like them, my dear?

Sir Buz. No, I don't like them, my dear; and who the devil did they come from, my dear? and to whom do they belong, my dear?

Lady Flip. Elegant manufacture!---nothing like it made in England.

Sir Buz. Where did they come from?

Lady Flip. Paris.

Sir Buz. Who owns them?

Lady Flip. They are your cloaths, my love!——

Sir Buz. Mine! Did you ever fee me wear fuch frippery?

Lady Flip. Yes, yours pofitively; but I did not intend you fhould have feen them—they were fmuggled.

Sir Buz. Smuggled!

Lady Flip. Yes, fmuggled from Paris, by my milliner, and fent here for the purpofe of ornamenting you, my fweet love!—

Sir Buz. Sweet love!—now that's fulfome— yet thou art my fweet love!

Lady Flip. Am I?---(*fmiling.*)

Sir

Sir Buz. Yes, like an apothecary's dofe,---
my bitter fweet.---

Lady Flip. How ill-natur'd!---but no matter, you fhall wear thefe cloaths at the ball this
evening.

Sir Buz. I will not.

Lady Flip. You fhall.

Sir Buz. Damn me if I do.

Lady Flip. Very well, Sir, then I'll fend
'em back.

Sir Buz. They fhall not be fent back, I
begin to like them,---a good colour, and not
too gaudy.---I'll keep them.

Lady Flip. Keep them!

Sir Buz. Yes, and wear them.

Lady Flip. Wear them,---where?

Sir Buz. At the ball this evening.---

Lady Flip. I fear you will take cold.

Sir Buz. You wifh I fhould take cold, but I
will not take cold,---and I will wear the
cloaths; you lay out a revenue on your back,
and I will, at leaft for this once, follow your
example.---I'll keep the cloaths, and go to the
ball in them this evening.

Lady Flip. (Afide.) The fmuggled cloaths
are fairly forfeited.

Enter G R A C E.

Grace. Dinner, my Lady!----*(feeing the
cloaths)* blefs me!

Lady Flip. (Apart.) Silence, all is well.---
Sir Buzzard you fee found the cloaths I ordered
Mrs. Muflin to procure him from Paris.

Grace. Well, I am fure, Sir, my Lady has
fitted you nicely, and I admire her tafte, that
I do; but will you wear them, Sir? *Sir*

Sir Buz. Yes, wear them, Sir!

Grace. Not 'till after dinner, Sir.

Sir Buz. Directly, Mrs. Prate,---I will furprize the company in them :---let dinner be kept back.

[*Exit* Sir Buzzard *with the cloaths.*

Grace. It was good luck he did not find the gentleman's fword---yet little matter if he had, for intriguing with an incumbrance about him; but how fhall I get him away?

Lady Flip. Poor foul! he muft have patience— contrive to convey him through the garden, to a chair, he may pretend he is a fervant taken ill, which will blind fufpicion.

[*Exit* Lady Flippant.

Grace. Well thought on,---my Lady's no fool, but fhe muft be a great fool indeed, who could not make a fool of a hufband.

[*Exit* Grace.

SCENE II,---*Ordeal's Houfe.*

Enter NICHOLAS *and* CLARA.

Nich. He, he, he, lack a daify, Mifs Clara--- the Scotchman looks gaily in his new cloaths, ---he is a brave youth,---what a leg *(looks at his leg)*---but I have got more of the calf.

Cla. Yes, a good deal more calf, Nicholas; ---but what can be the reafon that while he's teaching me, he fighs as piteoufly as if in pain,--- it goes to my heart to hear him without being able to give him eafe.

Nich. Why---why---ecod now, Mifs Clary, when you fpeak to me, it makes me figh, and gives me the heart-burn.

Cla.

Cla. What would you have me do, good Nicholas?

Nich. What would I have you do? I'll tell
you---ecod I cannot---but I'll tell you what the
Scotchman ought to do----he,---he ought.---

Cla. What!

Nich. Ecod, he ought to,----to---Sugar and
Honey!---what red lips you have!

Cla. What ought he to do?---

Nich. What ought he to do!---why he ought
to---how old are you?

Cla. Do not tantalize me, Nicholas.

Nich. Well, I will tell you, he ought to---
blefs my eyes, what a fine face fhe has!---he
ought to---he ought to---what pretty buckles
yours are!---he ought to,---well, fhake hands,
I will tell you *(takes her hand)* foft as fattin,---
he ought to---ecod, I fhould like to do it.

Cla. Do what?

Nich. I mean no offence---but he ought to---
(kiffes his hand) that's what he ought---

Cla. Oh, fhame, Nicholas,---fhame.

Nich. What fhame!---liften to me,---and I
won't go behind the bufh with you---my mafter
is a fool, and thinks nobody knows any thing but
himfelf---Now, when I fee a young man and a
young lady together,---and hear them figh, and
fee them ogle---why, I figh myfelf, and I---
I---ecod, I know what's what.

Cla. And what is it you know, Nicholas?

Nich. That the Scotch fcholard loves you,
and that you like the Scotch fcholard---I'ze been
in love, and I'ze never think of it, but---Oh,
but I can not tell you how it difturbs me---
(whiftles.)

Cla.

Cla. And I am difturbed too---heigh ho!

S O N G.

What wakes this new pain in my breaft?
  This fenfe that lay dormant before?
Lie ftill, bufy flutt'rer, and reft,
  The peace of my bofom reftore.

What wakes, &c.

Why trickles in filence the tear,
  This fighing---ah! what does it mean?
This mixture of hope and of fear,
  Where once all was mild and ferene.---

What wakes, &c.

Some pleafingly anxious alarm,
  Now warms and then freezes my heart,
Some foft irrififtible charm, .
  Alternate gives pleafure and fmart.

What wakes, &c.

Enter ORDEAL *and* DOUGLAS, *in a neat Scotch Drefs.*

Ord. Clara, your tutor tells me, you make an aftonifhing progrefs in your Grammar, and I am to hear you fpeak a leffon,---bring chairs, Nicholas *(they fit).*

Doug. Ha you got your Grammar, lady?

Cla. Yes, Sir, I have been ftudying my laft leffon *(takes a Grammar from her pocket).*

Doug. Be feated, lady, *(they fit).*

Ord. Modeft creature!---how the blufh mantles on her cheek!---don't be afhamed, Clary---Mac Claffic *(takes Douglas afide)* what a fub-

ject

ject for fpeculation---fhe is an orange tree, pof-
fefling at once the fprightly verdure of the
fpring, the fweet bloffom of the fummer, and
the ripe fruit of autumn. It revives me to look
on her.

Nich. It revives us to look on you.---

Ord. What think you of her eyes,---they
fhoot arrows of defire into the heart, but on her
lips lies an honied falve to heal the wound.

Doug. (agitated) Will you hear her repeat a
leffon?

Ord. See her mouth, a door of coral, opening
to a colonade of pearl.

Nich. Then her bofom, your honour.

Ord. Where the devil is the fellow going?
(fhakes him).

Doug. (afide) My fpirits are fo agitated, I
fhall betray myfelf.

Ord. Come, my lamb---begin.---there is a
mild creature, wax of my own fafhioning, and I
have moulded her into the very temper of my
affections.---

Nich. She can give you Latin for every thing
about you.

Ord. Reftrain your tongue, firrah. Go on
with your leffon, fweeteft, and never mind this
fellow.

Cla. (Tenderly) Amo, I love, *(looks at
Douglas)* amas, thou loveft, *(looks at Ordeal)*
amat, he loves!

Doug. (Sighs) Oh!

Cla. Amamus, we love. Oh! *(fighs)*

Nich. He, he, he, amo---I love!

Ord. Silence, rafcal!---but, Mac Claffic, are
the firft leffons in Lilly's grammar upon love?

Doug.

Doug. Aw grammars begin wi it, Sir---be-caufe love is the primœval principle of nature.

Nich. He, he, he!

Ord. Out of the room, you fcoundrel!

Nich. I go, zir. Amo, I love, amo, you love; amo, he loves, amo, we love,---he, he, he!

Exit Nicholas.

Doug. Shall we proceed, Sir.

Ord. If you pleafe.

Re-enter NICHOLAS.

Nich. There are three poor people below you defired to call.

Ord. I fhall return directly.---(*Nicholas following*) Where are you going? Stay here, ---Clara may want fomething---you'll give her a new leffon now, Mr. M'Claffick---I think fhe has got enough of amo and amas.

Exit Ordeal.

Nich. Zooks! he's jealous, zure as a gun, and left me here to watch you---but ecod, I'll be no fpoil-fport---fo teach away---I love, you love---he loves. *Exit* Nicholas.

Cla. What are you mufing on?---I like to hear your inftructions when we are alone.

Doug. (*afide*) To feduce fuch innocence would be damnable; when you are married to Mr. Ordeal, my inftructions will no longer pleafe,--- you love him?

Cla. I do indeed, as much as if he was my father,---but I never think of him when you are prefent.

Doug. Then you love him from gratitude?

Cla. Juft fo!---could I have any other mo-tive

tive ?---If there be any other kind of love, I wish you'd let me know it.

Doug. There is another kind,---give me your hand---there is a love known by its effects, it beats on the pulse, trembles on the breath, gives eyes to the thoughts, and thoughts to the eyes.

Cla. O la! then I'm sure you are in love, for your eyes speak and laugh,---why did you touch my hand?---indeed---indeed, I'm afraid I have taken it from you---I hope there's no danger in it.

Doug. Love is the child of desire, nurs'd by delight---weaned by inconstancy, consumed by neglect, kill'd by dissembling, and buried by ingratitude.

Cla. How cruel to kill it.

Doug. But then 'tis the parent of jealousy, the disuniter of friendship, and cause of disobedience; an arbitrary tyrant of the mind, that triumphs over wisdom, tramples upon prudence, and vanquishes even virtue.

Cla. O, you fright me with that description.

Doug. But where virtue is the basis of this passion, it produces the utmost happiness enjoyed on earth, and gives mortals a taste of heaven!

Cla. Now that is delightful! and to tell you the truth I have heard my guardian speak of it, but I could never feel it in his hand as I did in your's; he says---" love is fire full of cold---honey full of gall---and pleasure full of pain;"---but I see he knows nothing of the matter;---are you really in love?

Doug. Yes, my dear, deeply---deeeply;--- but why do you ask?

Cla. Because----

E

Doug.

Doug. Here comes Mr. Ordeal.

Cla. (*Aside*) I wish he was in Jericho.

Enter ORDEAL.

Ord. Very well---very well---here Nicholas! ---where's the rascal? Clara, my dear, seek him, and give orders for dinner, there's a good girl. (*Kisses her hand*).

Cla. Heigho! (*looks at Douglas*)---(*to Ordeal*) I obey, Sir.   *Exit* Clara.

Ord. An amiable, modest creature, Mr. M'Claffic---nothing ardent in her difpofition, has no more idea of love than an infant, yet a charming fertilizing conftitution, but chafte as ice,---" her heart like the falamander---cold, cold, in the midft of flame."

Doug. Virtue beams in her een, and animates her countenance; like the finifhing touches of the painter, it enlivens the portrait, and in-creafes the beauty of the object.

Ord. Poetically conceiv'd, and prettily pro-nounc'd;---yes, fhe fhrinks from the touch like the fenfitive plant---you have a prolific imagination, Mr. M'Claffic; confidering you come from a northern climate (*viewing Douglas*)---yet Mr. M'Claffic, there is no judging of a woman's chaftity, who has never been in the way of temptation.

Doug. Very true, Sir.

Ord. And women are virtuous in proportion to the temptations they withftand.

Doug. A juft conclufion, Sir.

Ord. Then you think it would be difficult to find a young inexperienced girl proof againft promifes, fighs and tears---and who could with-ftand the cunning infinuations of a lover.

                              Doug.

Doug. Certainly, Sir.

Ord. Well, I think differently; I think I could trust Clara---but she's a nonpareil---yes, cool as a cucumber in a hot bed---yet not prone to vegetation---but M'Claffic, I have an experiment to make, and you must affist me.

Doug. Command me, Sir.

Ord. Clara I think is a pure lamb.

Doug. Sir, there can be no doubt; but you were speaking of an experiment, Sir.

Ord. I have fortified her mind with morals, which will prove a shield to her by day, and a breast-plate by night.---But the experiment--- you must be my instrument.

Doug. In what respect, Sir?

Ord. To found the depth of her inclinations, ---to feel how the pulse of her affection beats towards me.

Doug. Sir!

Ord. If she should not like me---but that is a point for future confideration---if she should like me I will marry her in the morning.

Doug. Marry her, Sir!

Ord. Yes, marry her, Sir.

Doug. And in the morning. O my heart! and must I lose her after all?

Ord. In the morning---I have had a special licence sometime---yes, she loves me---I know she loves me---and soon as we have dined, I will go to Sir Buzzard's, to engage him and his friends to attend the ceremony In the mean time you must try the experiment---come in to dinner, and I'll give you further instructions.

Exeunt Ordeal *and* Douglas.

End of the THIRD ACT.

ACT IV.

ACT IV.

SCENE I. *Sir Buzzard's.*

Enter Sir BUZZARD *and* CHEATERLY. *Sir Buzzard in Welford's Cloaths.*

Cheat. CONSIDER, Sir Buzzard, we are in danger of a difcoveey every in-inftant.

Sir Buz. What can I do ?---Would you have me court the girl for you ? Befides, this bufinefs raifes a qualm in my confcience.

Cheat. Confcience!

Sir Buz. Yes, confcience!---my confcience cannot boaft fuch extenfive latitude and longitude as your's.---you have a convenient confcience, it ftretches or contracts like India rubber ; your confcience is a fervant of all work -- which you difcharge at a moment's warning.

Enter Colonel STAFF.

Col. May the fire of a platoon never again raife my fpirits, but it would be better for a man to attack a breach daily and on a forlorn hope, than to fit down before a coquet.

Cheat. " Have you ever attacked a breach, Colonel ?"

Sir Buz. You hear he has attacked a widow, and upon a forlorn hope."

Col. I fay, Sir, your fifter is a coquet.

Sir Buz. I fay fhe is a downright jilt. He who confides in the fex will be deceived---I defpife them.

Cheat. Yet keep a girl in a corner.

Sir Buz.

Sir Buz. " But not from affection to the girl,
I keep her becaufe it pleafes my humour, and
vexes my wife." You know the fex but fu-
perficially; there is my rib, when we married,
fhe was all delicacy and good humour, and from
her fmooth behaviour and oily tongue, I confi-
dered her a miracle of goodnefs. But the wind
foon veer'd about, and before the end of the
honey-moon blew a rank ftorm.

Col. " Talking of ftorms."

Sir Buz. " Hear me out---Upon refufing to
indulge her in fome fafhionable fubfcriptions,
there was a total eclipfe of the amiable, her
paffion fwell'd like a roaring fea, producing
nothing but fury, outrage and noife."

Enter ORDEAL *and* WIDOW.

Ord. I forgive you, madam,---I forgive you
---being determined to marry Clara in the morning.

Sir Buz. Ordeal, I underftand they have been
abufing you---but their beft friends cant 'fcape
their malignity---they have tongues of charcoal,
with which they are for ever blackening or burning characters.

Ord. I fhall immediately fet off with my
bride for London, from whence we will proceed on the grand tour.

Cheat. Have not I heard you exclaim againft
the grand tour.

Ord. You have heard me exclaim againft
fending our youth abroad without a proper controul. You have heard me fay, that on fuch
expeditions they too often contaminate their native virtue and conftitutions, by bartering the
honeft habits acquired in old England, for the

gew-

gew-gaw ornaments, and defpicable effeminacie of the Continent.

Wid. Pray, Mr. Ordeal, what retinue do you travel with ?

Cheat. The young Scotchman, Pure Nature's tutor, no doubt will make one.

Sir Buz. I wifh he may not make two ; I fpeak my mind, Ordeal.

Wid. What, the Colonel's friend ! fplit you through the crown ?

Col. She is at it again---madam, you fhould recolleét.

Wid. Then I fuppofe you will no longer re-ftrain her tafte in drefs---but allow her to throw off her prefent thin attire, and appear like a fa-fhionable chriftian,---in feathers and a hoop.

Ord. A hoop ! no---it makes a woman ap-pear like a walking fphere, encircled from the nadir to the meridian---and if the effeminacy of the men was not fo well known, one would be apt to imagine that the women were all in a ftate of---But I will not fpeak my mind now, ---though it is my way.

Enter a SERVANT.

Serv. Coffee is ferved in the faloon, madam.

Cheat. Have you feen Mifs Conftance ? *(afide to the fervant)*.

Serv. I believe, Sir, fhe is reading in the garden.   *Exit* Servant.

Ord. Sir Buzzard, I admire your drefs,---you look as fine---as---as the King of Pruffia in wax-work.

[*Exit* Ordeal.

Col. (To the widow) fhall I have the honor of your hand, Madam ?

                                       Wid.

Wid. No, Sir, I fhall never give my hand to a man who has loft my good opinion.

[*Exit* Widow.

Col. (*To Sir Buzzard*)---Do you hear that ?

Cheat. After her.

Sir Buz. After her purfe you mean.

Col. Capricious woman ! (*running turns round*) ---I once knew a Major---

Sir Buz. Know the Widow, man.---

Col. A Major in the forty-fecond. ·

Cheat. Away with you. (*they pufh him out*).

[*Exit* Colonel.

Cheat. You will excufe me to the ladies--- Conftance you hear is in the garden, I will feek her, and for the laft time plead my paffion, but if fhe perfeveres in rejecting my addreffes, I have your confent to carry her by ftratagem.

[*Exit* Cheaterly.

Sir Buz. Carry her off any way and I will be fatisfied.---   [*Exit* Sir Buzzard.

SCENE II.---*A Grotto:*

Conftance difcover'd fitting, fleeping, with a hand-kerchief over her face---a book near her.

Enter CHEATERLY.

Cheat. Afleep !---to difturb her would offend delicacy---and I muft footh her,---I will fit here till fhe wakes, here comes one of the fet-vants. (*Retires*).

Enter WELFORD. (*His fword under his arm.*)

Wel. How my landlady will laugh to fee me thus caparifon'd,---a woman fleeping, by the God of Love!---what a fortunate fellow am I!

---no sooner does one adventure vanish than another presents itself to my view---how gently she breathes,---the gale is reviving,---*(she sighs)* a sigh of sensibility,---poor soul!---it were pity she should sigh in vain. Yes, I will see her face. *(takes off the handkerchief)* O, Heaven's!----it is Constance---my life!---my heaven!---*(embraces her)*.

Con. Help!---oh, help!---

Enter CHEATERLY.

Cheat. Unhand the lady, villain!

Con. O, heavens, it is De Courcy!---

Wel. Ha! is it you? I have met my blessing and my curse.

Cheat. De Courcy!---

Wel. I have been your dupe, Sir, and I know it.---Am well inform'd of those combinations by which you defrauded me,---and am determin'd, Sir, to give the law it's course.

Cheat. I scorn to retort your assertions,---you have been a dupe to your own folly. Pride, and high founding language but ill suit with the meanness of your appearance, assumed for the purpose of some low intrigue,---metamorphose into a gentleman, and I'll enforce satisfaction for this insolence.   [*Exit* Cheaterly.

Con. O, I shall faint.

Well. My dear love,---pardon the momentary neglect into which passion led me.---I have been but one day in England---tomorrow I should have gone for York,---my soul was all impatience to see you.---

Con. What, in a livery!

Wel. A livery---yes,---it is a disguise I own, worn for a purpose I'll not attempt to palliate

or

or juftify---but your appearance like a heavenly
vifion infpires me with virtuous thoughts.

Con. I do not urge an explanation which muft
increafe your confufion.

Wel. I will explain all another time.---Here
comes fome of the family.

Enter Sir BUZZARD *and* ORDEAL.

Sir Buz. Thefe alarms will ruin my conftitution,---it was fortunate I took bark this morning, or my whole nervous fyftem would be
fhaken to pieces.---Where is this gentleman?---
Cheaterly tells me a ftranger has been rude to
you, have you turn'd him out, Patrick?

Con. (*To Ordeal*) Sir, I fhall fend a letter to
your houfe immediately, to which I implore
your attention---I am wretched, you were my
father's friend.

Ord. Madam, if I was not, I am a man, and
every thing that affects my fellow-creatures
concerns me.   [*Exit* Conftance.

Sir Buz. Patrick,---do you hear?---no anfwer,
---I fhall never recover my health,---don't ir-
ritate me, rafcal.---

Wel. Rafcal!---to whom do you addrefs yourfelf?

Sir Buz. To you, fcoundrel.---

Wel. Why, you defpicable,---that epithet
again, and this fword.---

Sir Buz. This is no Irifhman!---what the devil is become of your brogue?---who are you?

Wel. A gentleman!---

Ord. A gentleman! ha, ha, ha, this is good!
---a gentleman in a livery!---but which are you?
                              a gen-

a gentleman in waiting, or a gentleman of the road?

Sir Buz. Ah, ah! I now fee how I came by the new fuit, fmuggled from Paris.

Ord. The fervant is mad, and Sir Buzzard has caught the contagion.

Sir Buz. I have it here. (*Striking his head.*)

Ord. What have you there?

Wel. Nothing that I know of, upon my honor.

Ord. Nothing in your mafter's head! How dare you joke with your betters, young man?

Sir Buz. I fhall be the laughing-ftock of fools and jeft of the malignant.

Enter G R A C E.

Grace. Oh, dear, dear, fure there is no harm done! It is all my fault,---Mifs Conftance is ready to break her heart;---you muft know, Sir, I was the only perfon in the houfe who knew this gentleman, he is her lover, and he wheedled me, and wheedled me, till I confented to bring him into the houfe, and fo I fhut him into my lady's clofet.

Wel. The girl tells the truth.

Ord. He is a gentleman, and you fhut him up in your lady's clofet. (*To Sir Buzzard.*) Now, I fee what you conceive in your head.

Grace. And fo, Sir, my lady coming in, the gentlemen was oblig'd to lie clofe.

Sir Buz. And he wheedled you, and wheedled you,---" And he lay clofe,---Eh"---and he never faw your lady?

Grace. Never faw her, as I hope to be faved!

Wel. You hear the girl fwear.

Ord.

Ord. O, it's plain there was nothing between them.

Grace. " Nothing between them indeed, Sir, that is the naked truth."   [*Exit* Grace. .

Sir Buz. Then give me leave, Sir, to enquire who you are ? and what are your pretenfions. to vifit my niece ?

Wel. As to my pretenfions, Sir, nothing can be better founded,---I love the lady,---but what is ftill more material, the lady has long fince confefs'd that fhe loves me.

Ord. Candid and open.

Sir Buz. And your name is De Courcy ?

Wel. To that name I was born, but an old good natured uncle taking it into his head to vifit elizium---in obedience to his will, and in gratitude for fixteen hundred pounds a year, I now bear the name and arms of Welford.

Ord. You feem an honeft fellow, worthy the love of Conftance.

Sir Buz. What is his honefty to me ? I am to inform you, Sir, the father of Conftance is dead; I am her natural guardian, and you fhall never have my confent to marry her.

Wel. May I never obtain her confent, if ever I afk ycurs.

Sir Buz. She has not a fhilling fortune.

Wel. I am glad of it, I have fufficient fortune for both, --I will fettle a fortune on her.

Ord. A fellow of noble generofity !---

Sir Buz. There is a gentleman, I am determined fhe fhall marry.

Wel. Mark me,---let that gentleman be whom he may, If he prefumes to fpeak to her, write to her,---or even thinks of her as a wife, I fhall

make.

make him such an example---but this is losing
time,---farewell, I must wait on Constance.

(going.)

Sir Buz. (*Opposing him.*) You shall not go
an inch into my house,---that is your way out.

Wel. I will go into any man's house, Sir,
where she is,---debar me access to my love!---
Were you the Grand Signor, and detain'd her,
I would force into the inmost recesses of your
seraglio, put you to death in the midst of your
Janissaries, and carry her off in triumph.

Ord. I do not often swear, it is not my way,
but damn me if I would not assist you.

Sir Buz. Nay, then we must try your courage, (*lays his hand upon his sword*)---O, for an
estringent to brace my nerves.

Wel. Excuse me from running you through
the body while you wear my cloaths ; that coat
is in excellent taste, and I cannot think of
running it through the body.---

Ord. A soldier, and a wit!

Sir Buz. Take it, take it ; (*throws off* Welford's *coat*)---now let me see if you get
into my house. (*draws.*)

Ord. What, going to fight a duel !---Oh, for
shame !---duelling is a mode of satisfaction
unworthy gentlemen, practis'd now by every
vulgar fellow ;----people of fashion should ex-
plode it.

Sir Buz. (*Trembling.*) You know I pay great
respect to your opinion,---and if,---but he shall
not go into my house.

Ord. Consider what an improper place for
quarreling.

Well. You are right, Sir, this is too cold a
situation for stripping ;---(*takes up the cloaths*
and

and hands them to Ordeal.) now for Conſtance,
love, and happineſs.　[*Exit* Welford, *running*.

Ord. Bravo, my boy!---bravo!

Sir Buz. Sure ſome malign devil has determin'd to make me ridiculous!---let me after
him. *(Ordeal holds him.)*

Enter Lady FLIPPANT, MUSLIN, *and* GRACE.

Lady Flip. Are you mad, Sir Buzzard?

Sir Buz. Stark mad!

Ord. Nearly ſtark naked mad.

Sir Buz. The cloaths,---the ſmuggled cloaths
you provided for me.

Lady Flip.
Ord. } Ha, ha, ha!

Sir Buz. Away! you old——get home;---
perhaps your Scotch tutor may prepare Pure
Nature for the grand tour, and provide you
more company than you expeƈt.----Why did I
marry?---why plunge into a mortal diſeaſe, for
which there is no remedy but poiſon,---no re-
lief but death?　　　　　[*Exit* Sir Buzzard.

Ord. Can I ſee Conſtance?

Lady Flip. She is lock'd up in her own apart-
ment to avoid her lover.

Ord. To avoid him!---He is a noble fellow,
and ſhe muſt have him;---I will in to Sir Buzzard, and argue this caſe:---He preſumes to
controul this young lady, his niece, by parental authority; but I will convince him, the
principle of that authority is to make our children or wards happy,---not miſerable.

[*Exit* Ordeal.

Muſ. Sir Buzzard is in a horrid rage.

Lady Flip. I muſt contrive to appeaſe him.
Conſtance I ſuppoſe has her ſuſpicions;---an
　　　　　　　　　　　　　　　amiable

amicable girl---I really love her, pity her situation, and am determined never to see Welford again, but for the purpose of facilitating a marriage between them.---I must also effectuate a breach between my sister and this pusilanimous colonel.

Muf. That may be easily accomplished---the widow has no small share of vanity.

Lady Flip. True!---

Muf. We must perfuade her she was the object of Mr. Welford's admiration.

Grace. I will swear he brib'd me to introduce him to her.

Muf. And I will contrive to get her and the gentleman together at my house, and your ladyship shall send the Colonel to surpirze them, which will produce an irreconcileable quarrel.

Lady Flip. Here comes the widow---do you lay the train.

Enter the widow VOLATILE.

Wid. De Courcy is gone, after a very loud altercation with Cheaterly, which terminated in mutual vows of vengeance; he charges Cheaterly with having imposed on him at play.

Lady Flip. There is nothing scandalous in that ---play has become a science, fashionable in practice, and like other *faux pas*, 'tis only blameable in discovery. Pray how has Constance behaved?

Wdi. Remains locked up in her own room, and perseveres in denying an interview to her lover:---this De Courcy is in my opinion a charming fellow.

Lady Flip. But I must know for what purpose he was brought into my closet.---I am certain Constance was not the object; so speak, Grace.

Grace.

/

Grace. Well, my lady, the truth is, the gentleman came after the widow.

Lady Flip. I thought fo,----this duplicity, fifter, hurts me.

Grace. Dear, my lady, it is all my fault,--- the gentleman faw Mrs. Volatile at the play with your ladyfhip, and fent for me in the morning--- and,---but am I fure of pardon if I tell ?

Lady Flip. Yes, if you tell nothing but the truth.

Grace. Well, my lady, the poor young gentleman to be fure fwore bitterly he was fmitten ; ---by all the Gods, fays he, fhe is one of the moft beautifuleft,---moft youngeft, and moft eleganteft creatures my eyes ever beheld f---but I, telling him as how fhe was pofitively engaged to colonel Staff,---then he began to curfe.——

Wid. Why prefume to tell him fo ?---Who gave you knowledge of my engagements?

Lady Flip. Hear the girl, fifter ; *(afide)* fhe's caught.

Grace. Do'nt be angry, madam,---I told him, madam---thinking no harm, and fo he curs'd, and call'd on Heaven, and poor gentleman figh'd fo, that I took pity on him, and by his perfuafions and promifes brought him into the clofet, where he was to have been concealed,--- Yes, ma'am---'till I could have contriv'd to have brought you into the room, which I fhould have done, but that my lady firft came, and then Sir Buzzard, who made up the noife that difturb'd the houfe.

Lady Flip. You are an impudent girl, go wait in my dreffing-room 'till my coming.

Grace. Yes, my lady,---but oh, fure, you do'nt intend to difcharge me,---what could I do

when

when fo pretty a gentleman knelt to me, and cried to me for affiftance---and fqueez'd my hand, and forc'd a purfe into my bofom---Oh! oh! *(crying, apart to the widow)*---you will fpeak to my lady.

Wid. I will, Grace! *(apart)* there *(gives money)*--- let me fee you prefently.

Exit Grace, *laughing.*

A pretty fcheme this!---your maid, Lady Flippant, has ufed me well---did I ever make any pofitive engagements with the Colonel?

La. Flip. I hope not, but really you take fuch pains to torment each other, I was apprehenfive you were privately married.

Wid. Heav'n forbid!---I have been prudently confidering the Colonel's fituation fome time paft---his eftate I underftand has been long languifhing in a decline, and his creditors no doubt are in expectation of mine.

La. Flip. Then to beftow it on Welford---think of the pleafure of fweet five and twenty fmiling upon you from morning 'till night.

Muf. And from night to morning---think of that, madam.

La. Flip. Then our triumph over a girl of fuch beauty as Conftance---the buz of the polite world, and their impertinent ill-nature.

Wid. Certainly there are inducements.

La. Flip. Inducements! you will have the exquifite fatisfaction of being lampoon'd, epigramm'd, and paragraph'd---or perhaps be etch'd in aqua fortis, and ftuck up in the print fhops. Then to have the tribe of antiquated maidens, difgufted wives, and difappointed widows railing at your prudence, yet envying
your

your fituation---" Lord blefs us!"---ejaculates
Lady Toothlefs, " I wonder at her indifcretion,
to marry a man fo young. The Colonel would
have been much more fuitable."---Then fhe
takes five years from your lover's age, and adds
to your's---" That's he!---that's he!"---ex-
claims Mifs Squintum, as fhe ogles from a fide
box, with one eye worn out in fearching for
defects in beauty, and the other on the decline
---" That's he,---but I cannot perceive what
fhe faw in the fellow; he is as plain as herfelf
---and I wonder how women can follow fellows."---The blooming youth hands you to
your feat--the whole circle ftare at you--a general whifper's breath'd round--you gaze in return
with perfect compofure---falute your acquaint-
ance---adjuft your tucker, giggle behind your
fan, affume a perfect indifference, whifper your
handfome hufband to mortify them, and laugh
out to fhew your inward fatisfaction and ineffa-
ble contempt.

Wid. But how is all this to be brought about?

Muf. Call at my houfe within an hour, and
if I do not fettle it, difcard me from your confidence. ——

Lady Flip. She fhall be punctual—come,
fifter, I fee you were unacquainted with your
lover's paffion,--but you muft acknowledge
I had fufficient caufe for fufpicion.

Wid. Yet you muft allow there was no deceit
on my part.   [*Exit* Widow.

Muf. You have play'd your part admirably.

Lady Flip. Yes, Muflin, all good actreffes
are not upon the ftage.

[*Exeunt* Lady Flippant *and* Muflin.

F   SCENE

SCENE III. *Ordeal's House.*

Enter Douglas, Clara, *and* Nicholas.

Nich. You are no longer a Scotchman I zee——

Doug. Yes, Nicholas, I have only laid aside the tone and accent, but am still a Scotchman; I have no reason to be ashamed of my country, and I trust my country will never have reason to be ashamed of me.

Nich. Why zee master, I could never zee any difference between your English and Scotch; though to be zure I could hear it in their speaking, and that is the only difference I think should ever be between them; but take a fool's advice now,---make the best use of your time.

Exit Nicholas.

Doug. What employs your thoughts, my love?

Cla. In truth, love itself; if the pleasing description you have given me be true, and I have no reason to doubt your veracity, to live with those we love must be the extent of human happiness ;---but then, Mr. Ordeal has told me that your sex often requite the most sincere passion with cold indifference.

Doug. The charge is too true; but my affection can only cease with life.

Cla. I owe every thing to Mr. Ordeal's goodness, and the very arguments you urged to gain my love, persuade me against being ungrateful!---obedience is the only return I can make his kindness, and how can I disobey him, when my heart informs me that ingratitude is

one of thofe heinous fins at which Heaven is moſt
offended ?

Doug. It is true, no quality of the foul is
more lovely than gratitude ;---but Mr. Ordeal
is not actuated by paffion,---he offers you his
hand from motives of generofity, not love,---all
you owe him is friendſhip, which an union with
me could not diminiſh.

Cla. You can perfuade me to any thing ;---
vou fwear you love me,---I believe you,---and
if the pleafure I take in feeing you, and hearing
you, and the pain I feel when you leave me,
be love, I love you above all things.

Re-enter N i c h o l a s.

Nich. Have you fettled every thing ?
Doug. Good Nicholas, do not interrupt her.
Nich. Who, I, a fpoil-fport ! mum !——
                              [*Exit* Nicholas.

Cla. Would not my confenting to marry you
be injuſtice to my benefactor ?
Doug. The value I fet upon your love is fuch,
I would not accept it, but as the voluntary gift
of your foul !---I will obtain Mr. Ordeal's confent.

Cla. Then I am for ever yours. *(He kiffes her
hand.)*

Enter O r d e a l *and* N i c h o l a s.

Ord. (afide)---What do I fee !
Cla. But when will you obtain his confent ?
Ord. Never.
Cla. O, we are undone.
Ord. (to Douglas) Is this the way you repay
my confidence ? and you, *(to Clara)* innocent

mifs, is this a grateful return for years of kindnefs?---But *(to Nicholas)* what fhall I fay to
you, rafcal!---you, whom I thought watchful as
a lynx, have flumber'd like another Argus---
were your eyes piped into a nap by this Mer-
cury, or was your mouth ftopped by a fop, Mr.
Cerberus?

Nich. Yes, I loves a fop;---but I will be
called no names---zee mafter,---our bargain is
this, a month's warning, or a month's wages;
zo, pay me, and I'll go, but remember it was
not I brought maifter M'Claffic into the houfe.

[*Exit* Nich.

Doug. Your refentment, Sir, muft fall folely
upon me---I only have deceiv'd you,---a word
in private,---*(takes Ordeal afide)* could human
nature repel the influence of fuch beauty?---
(points to Clara) had I been lefs honourable, or
Clara lefs virtuous, I might now perhaps be
impofing upon your credulity a feduced maid,
with a vitiated mind: I am young,---Clara is
pure nature,---the experiment I have made was
dangerous.———

Ord. But you were only to have made the experiment to try how far her inclinations coincided
with mine.

Doug. Confider, fhe was an orange tree.---

Ord. You were to have been the inftrument
for promoting my happinefs.

Doug. She poffefs'd the verdure of the
fpring———

Ord. Hear me!

Doug. The bloffom of the fummer———

Ord. Hear me!

Doug. The ripe fruit of autumn.

Ord. And you would confider me the falling
leaf in winter---hear me, Sir!---*(loud)* Have

you

you not been urging the temptations of pleafure to feduce her into your own defigns ?---have you not alienated her affections from me ?

Doug. Sir, I came into your houfe for the very purpofe of gaining her love.

Ord. Who are you, Sir ?

Doug. A foldier---my name Douglas,---my fortune a competency,--my country Scotland---the fame perfon who affifted you when attack'd by ruffians on Marlborough Downs.

Cla. The kind gentleman in whofe arms I fainted !

Doug. From the firft inftant I faw her, my foul caught the infpiration of virtuous love.

Ord. You are unfafhionable, Sir,---from the diffipated converfation of the young fellows of the times, one would imagine there was neither honefty in man, nor chaftity in woman ;---but your conduct contradicts their afperfions.

Doug. It is too true, the arts of feduction are fo feduloufly ftudied, that honeft love appears in danger of being extirpated.

Ord. There are many, many melancholy examples ;----but be affured, young man, though fenfual pleafures arife from feducing innocence, it is plucking bloffoms from a fweet-briar, which will rankle in the flefh.

Doug. Your obfervation, Sir, is juft,---though it does not apply to me.------

Ord. " My cenfure does not fall folely on youth,---no, the gardens of beauty and innocence are alfo defpoil'd by old debilitated wretches, who cannot cultivate the foil, but lay wafte its beauties.",

Cla. Do you forgive me, Sir ?

Ord.

Ord. I blame you not, I am your debtor for many inftances of duty and affection;--- look on her, Douglas;——yet her beauty is the leaft of her excellence,——but as it is a principal part of benevolence to affift another moft when there is moft need of affiftance, ---and that you need not owe too much to the generofity of your hufband,---as you cannot be my wife, I adopt you for my child---love infpires its votaries with fentiment, and I acknow= ledge the benign influence. (*Joins their hands.*)

Doug. You weep, my lovely Clara!

Ord. And fo do you,---and fo do I,——— I fee you are all joy,——but, my children, the tranfports of a virtuous paffion are the leaft parts of its happinefs,---we will this inftant to Sir Buzzard Savage's,---a young lady, his niece, calls for my protection,

Doug. You mean Conftance Heartfree! young De Courcy, of York, my particular friend, is, I believe, betrothed to her.———

Ord. You are right;---take your bride by the hand;---the women will laugh at me for lofing her, but I am above the laugh of the world, and I will laugh at the world in my turn,--that is my way.——— *Exeunt.*

End of the FOURTH ACT.

ACT.

A C T. V.

SCENE I. *Lady Flippant's Dressing Room.*

Enter LADY FLIPPANT.

Lady Flip. THE storm bends this way, and here will I meet it. (*Sits down, and takes a book.*)

Enter Sir BUZZARD *and* GRACE.

Sir Buz. (*Pushing Grace before him*) you shall instantly march out of my house. (*Pushes her.*)

Grace. My lady scorns your suspicions.

Sir Buz. Stop your gabble, you diminitive pandar in petticoats!---It is clear that Constance was ignorant of Welford's arrival in England!---it is apparent he did not come to my house after her.---What, is your noble blood at a loss for an excuse?

Lady Flip. Who has instilled jealousy into that head of yours, barren of every thing but what is monstrous! (*Reads.*)

Sir Buz. It is your Ladyship has made my head monstrous.

Enter Colonel STAFF.

Col. Sure the devil instigates some women!--- the widow——

Sir Buz. Do not throw the blame on the poor *devil*---it is nature instigates them, and she is to the full as subtle and certain in her operations.

Col. I just now spoke to her as she stept out of a chair into Mrs. Muslin's, and in return was

shot

ſhot through the heart with a look of ill-nature
and contempt——if I was not the cooleſt fellow
in the ſervice, I'd run mad,---aye,--mad, mad---

Lady Flip. You would have cauſe to run mad,
if you knew ſhe is now at Mrs. Muſlin's, en-
joying a tete-a-tete with Welford.

Col. Impoſſible!

Grace. I am ready to take my oath of it!
(*to Sir Buzzard*) the truth is, I told a great
lie to your honour.

Sir Buz. O, confound me, but I believe
you now.   [*Exit* Grace.

Col. The widow gone to Welford, on an
aſſignation---ha! ha! ha! I will after her this
inſtant, and cut his throat!---No, I will not
ſtir- -I am pleas'd---perfectly pleas'd!---I will
diſcharge ſuch a volley about his ears;---gone
to viſit Welford!--but why ſhould I be vex'd?-
I will follow her, ſpring a mine, and blow them
up together---Burſt on her like a hand-granade.

Lady Flip. Ridiculous----you are all gun-
powder.

Col. Ungrateful woman!

Sir Buz. Deceitful ſex!

Lady Flip. Surprize her and her lover!

Col. I will break with her——I mean I will
purſue her.   [*Exit.*

Lady Flip. Well, you ſee it was your ſiſter,
not your wife, Welford came to viſit; are
you ready to make an apology for your vulgar
ſuſpicions?

Sir Buz. An apology to you! O, impudence!
have you not been the ruſt of my health, have
you not fretted me down to a mere ſkeleton?

                                              make

make you an apology !---give me my wasted flesh.

Lady Flip. I shall for London in the morning.

Sir Buz. If you dare !

Lady Flip. Will shew out at every place of public entertainment.

Sir Buz. At your peril.

Lady Flip. At your cost.

Sir Buz. The law gives me authority to confine you, and I will exercise it---I am your husband.

Lady Flip. I am heartily sorry for it !- will have public breakfasts, public dinners, and public nights.

Sir Buz. You shall have bread and water, in a narrow room.

Lady Flip. A box at the Opera, and subscribe to all the Concerts.

Sir Buz. You devil !

Lady Flip. Will purchase a new vis-a-vis--- a town chariot and phaeton.

Sir Buz. You---you have a design upon my life.

Lady Flip. Heav'ns ! how ardently I pant to be elevated in the phaeton, to take the circuit of Hyde Park, rolling in a cloud of dust, four horses, two outriders, whip in hand, flowing manes, hunters tails, sweep down Piccadilly, turn into St. James's-street,---up fly the club-house windows, out pop the powderedheads of the bucks and beauxs of fashion--some nod, some smile, some kiss hands,---all praise---she is a goddess, exclaims one,---a venus, ejaculates another,---an angel, sighs a third. I cut on, flash

down

down Pall Mall fwift as lightning, rattle furioufly through Charing-Crofs, overturn Lady Dapper's whim and cats at Northumberland Houfe, lofe a wheel in the Strand, leap from my feat as the carriage falls, and am received in the arms of fome handfome fellow whom love has directed to my affiftance.

Sir Buz. She is mad! fhe is mad! outrageous mad!

Lady Flip. He carries me into a houfe, fainting——

Sir Buz. Stop there; I will be divorc'd.

Lady Flip. Then I will have a feparate maintenance.

Sir Buz. Not a fhilling.

Lady Flip. You cannot deprive me of my fettlement.

Sir Buz. Ay, there is the grievance! O, confound all jointures and fettlements, thofe encourage your levities, and ftimulate you all to tranfgrefs.   [*Exit* Sir Buzzard.

Lady Flip. (*Sits.*) My poor fpirits are exhaufted! Heigh ho! I am tired of this diffipated life.

Enter CONSTANCE.

Con. I wait upon your ladyfhip, to return grateful thanks for the many favours you have conferred upon me, and to take my leave, as I am determined to quit this houfe.

Lady Flip. What! without your uncle's confent?

Con. I cannot think his confent neceffary, while he and your ladyfhip affent to the perfecution I experienced from a man I defpife.

Lady

Lady Flip. (*Rifing*) And pray where do you intend to go ?

Con. I have found a protector---Mr. Ordeal, the friend of my unfortunate father. Lady. Flippant, it hurts my heart to part you upon thofe terms. (*Weeps and walks as going.*)

Lady Flip. In tears, Conftance ! (*Conftance returns*) Why fo diftrefs'd ?

Con. My heart is too full.

Lady Flip. Be feated ; (*they fit*) you love this Mr. Welford fincerely---but he is ! (*afide*) what is it to me what he is ! (*Rifes*)

Con. To me he is every thing---and it is my hope !---(*rifes*)---but why fhould I hope ?---

Lady Flip. Conftance-- I really love you---our manners have divided us ; but be affured, my dear girl, though I run the circle of fafhionable life, my mind is not devoid of fenfibility---our education has been different.

Con. It was my happinefs to receive inftruction from a pious and tender mother, who early taught me the precepts of virtue, and imprefled upon my heart, that a pure reputation with humble poverty, was preferable to a fufpicious character, though blazoned with all the pomp and ornaments of elevated life---but fhe is no more.

Lady Flip. (*Rifes*) Alas, Conftance! it was my misfortune to be educated in all the giddy foibles and levities of the times.

Con. (*Rifes*) But I have obferved a difpofition in your ladyfhip fufceptible of the tendereft offices of friendfhip,---and where there is feeling---

Lady Flip. There is hope of reformation---you would have faid fo---indeed, Conftance, there

there are sentiments here, which often upbraid me; but sure nothing has transpir'd, injurious to my honour.

Con. The world is censorious, madam, and those whose conversation is the most entertaining are often the most dangerous; to simplicity they impute cunning, and give a criminal construction to the most innocent actions.

Enter ORDEAL *and* CLARA.

Ord. I am all joy, Lady Flippant! Constance, this is Clara, hereafter I trust you will be inseparable friends.

Clara. I shall endeavour to merit the lady's friendship.

Ord. They may boast of Queen Emma walking over burning ploughshares, but here is a girl has done more, she has lived in a fashionable family without censure. (*Takes Constance by the hand.*)

Lady Flip. But, Mr. Ordeal, what is the cause of your joy?

Ord. It must be disclos'd---Pure Nature has bestowed her hand and heart on the Scotch lad, who turns out to be Captain Douglas, Welford's intimate friend.

Con. Sir, I know the gentleman, and he bears a high character.

Lady Flip. Constance, take this young lady to the drawing-room, send Grace to me, and order your maid over to Welford's, to let him know you will be there presently. I have a serious reason for my request, and will not be denied.

Con. I obey.　　　[*Exeunt* Constance *and* Clara.
Lady

Lady Flip. The poor girl's situation is truly pitiable---it was our subject when you came in----the tears are not yet out of my eyes.

Ord. Never blush for weeping ; tears are the certain symptoms of a noble soul.

Lady Flip. Do you know that I have serious thoughts of throwing aside all fashionable levities ?

Ord. I know it is almost time ; I believe your inclinations are virtuous, and your irregularities I do not impute to nature ;---no, my lady, nature has endowed you with amiable qualities, among which, I think generosity is prevalent--- like most of your sex, you have taken up levity through whim, and maintain it through habit, though perhaps your soul struggles to be delivered from the trammels ;--break them, then, and you will do more than Cæsar ;---he conquered countries,---but the greatest glory human nature can acquire is to conquer ourselves ;---I have good news for Constance,---her father is living.

Lady Flip. Heav'ns !---are you serious ?

Ord. I have had letters from London, and he returns by the next ships from India ;---- nay more,---he has remitted thirty thousand pounds to her sole use, with directions to prepare a house for his reception.

Lady Flip. O, I am overjoy'd---why has she never heard from him before ?

Ord. He was sent upon an embassy to the interior parts of the country, and his letters were intercepted and destroyed.---But seriously, has your ladyship known nothing of this before ?

Lady Flip. Never.

Ord.

Ord. There is roguery on foot,---an expreſs was ſent to your ſeat at York, which not meeting the lady there was forwarded to this city, and delivered at this houſe.

Lady Flip. I ſee into it, this accounts for the warm impetuous paſſion of Cheaterly; the girl and her fortune were no doubt to be ſacrificed, between him and my worthy ſpouſe. Then you muſt aſſiſt me in perſuading Conſtance to go to Welford; it will produce an incident which will puniſh the young gentleman's paſſion for intrigue, and give Conſtance an authority over him; *(going, returns)* but do you believe my repentance ſincere?

Ord. I hope ſo !---but I believe nothing without proof---that is my way---where there is levity the world will ſuſpect, and when the world has once cauſe to ſuſpect a woman, her character becomes as much the ſport of its malice, as if there was a certainty of her having abandoned it.

Lady Flip. I am penitent! but do you really forgive my lecture to Pure Nature?

Ord. Yes, and am convinc'd you are no falſe prophet; for, as you foretold, Clara preferred the ſummer dimples of youth to the winter wrinkles of age,---I ſpeak my mind, that is my way.

[*Exeunt* Ordeal *and* Lady Flippant.

SCENE II. *Mrs. Muſlin's.*

The WIDOW, *Mrs.* MUSLIN, *and* WELFORD, *diſcovered at Tea.*

Wel. Your opinion, madam, is juſt! vivacity is an attribute to woman,----gravity natural to man :---and probably the fexes were thus contrafted, that the faturnine difpofition of the male might be relieved by the fprightlinefs of the female,---vour fmiles alleviate our pains, your approbation rewards our dangers.

Wid. And our converfation illuftrates my opinion---you are grave,---I, perhaps, too volatile.

Muf. The poor gentleman feems as if fomething preyed upon his mind ;---let me recommend matrimony,---it is the only cure for melancholy.

Wel. And often a fpecific for all complaints,

Muf. Well,---bufinefs muft be minded *(going.)*

Wel. *(Rifes.)* Muft fee you to the door.

Muf. *(Afide.)* A great fortune,---may I truft her with you?

Wel. May I truft myfelf with *her?* *(afide.)*
                           [*Exit Mrs.* Muflin.

A good, merry, convenient, civil old woman :--- fhe recommends matrimony---*(fits.)* Pray, madam, what kind of lover would you prefer?

Wid. I muft tell you the lover I would not prefer. I would not prefer a coxcomb,---a fluttering fummer infect,---a talkative creature, full of infipid gefture, laughter, and noife, who pays more attention to his hair than to his intellects,--- who poffeffes neither fentiment for friendfhip, nor fenfibility for love---but is curft with a foul devoid of manlinefs, and bent on the gratification of its own puny affections.

Wel. An excellent picture, yet the fpecies of animal you defcribe are favorites.------The ladies are grown fo enamoured of delicate limbs, and effeminate faces, one would imagine they wifhed to have their lovers women in every thing.

Enter

Enter Mrs. M U S L I N.

Muf. Dear Sir, there is a woman below enquiring for you---fhe infifts upon coming up,
and has fuch a tongue!

Wid. I would not be feen for the world.

Muf. She would furely blaft the reputation of
my houfe.---Sir, you muft go down to her.---
O my poor character!   [*Exit Mrs.* Muflin.

Wel. Any thing to fave the reputation of
your houfe. (*Going.*)

Enter Mrs. M U S L I N.

Muf. Madam, madam, the flut is upon the
ftairs.---Step into this clofet till the impudent
creature is gone.---(*Puts the widow in the clofet*)
You do not know, Sir, you have been fitting with
Mrs. Volatile, fifter to Sir Buzzard Savage.

Honor. (*Within*) Mr. Welford.

Wel. I know that voice.

Muf. It is the clack of Mrs. Honor, waiting-
maid to Mifs Conftance.

Welf. Then keep her out for Heaven's fake.

Hon. (*Within*) I will have admittance.

Muf. Coming, Mrs. Honor.——O the audacious wretch---I fee, Sir, you are a man of
gallantry, but, pray, difpatch the creature as
faft as poffible. |*Exit.* Muf.

Hon. (*Within*) Madam I infift upon going in
firft.

Grace. (*Within*) No me'm—you will pardon
me.

Enter GRACE *and* HONOR *pufhing in together.*

Wel. What, two!——ladies, your moft obedient.——(*bows——they curtfey*)

Hon.

Hon. You have no bufinefs here, me'm,———

Grace. My bufinefs, me'm, is no bufinefs of your's——or if it was your bufinefs, me'm, yet it is not the bufinefs of the likes of you to look down upon the likes of me, me'm.

Hon. The likes of you I look down upon with fcorn.——It is not for the likes of you, to look up to the likes of me, me'm.——I ferves a lady of vartue.

Grace. Vartue! Your infinuation is low, me'm, high as you carry your head.

Wel. Grace, ftand on my right hand—Honor, take your place on my left—How happy would it be for England, were all her great men in my fituation---Grace fupporting one fide. Honor fupporting the other.---Now, ladies, to the caufe of your vifit.

Grace. My lady underftanding that } her fifter was here—— } *together.*

Hon. My Lady fent me to let you } know—— }

Wel. One at a time.

Grace. Sir, you muft know—} *together.*

Hon. My lady fent—— }

Wel. Here is a guinea for her who fpeaks *fecond*——What, dumb!——but money feals as well as unfeals the mouths of great fpeakers.

Hon. Me'm, I fhall certainly fpeak firft—Sir, you muft know——

Grace. Speak firft, me'm! I ferve a lady of quality.

Wel. Order in the houfe——let me fettle this point of precedence---I believe it is regular that Grace fhould take the lead of Honor, fo Mrs. Grace begin.

G

Hon.

Hon. Thank you for preferring fhe.

(Walks about.)

Wel. Now Grace, what is your bafinefs with me ?

Grace. La, Sir, I have no bufinefs with *you* -- I want to fpeak with Mrs. Volatile.

Wel. Child, fhe is not here.

Grace. Not *here*---but I believe fhe is *there*

(points to clofet.)

Wel. By this guinea fhe is not. *(gives money.)*

Grace. By this guinea I will fwear it---mum--- but my lady wants to fee her directly---Mrs. Honor, your very obedient---an audacious huf- fey!--- *(afide.)* [*Exit* GRACE.

Hon. Me'm, your moft humble----- *(afide.)* Lord, Sir, I found it as difficult to get at you, as if you had been a great Turk.

Wel. Mrs. Muflin did not know you perhaps.

Hon. Not know me ! fhe knew me to be var- tuous, though as the faying is, " tell me your company and I will tell you what you are"----- and I, and my miftrefs live in a family where there is not much vartue practifed---but I am filent---fervants fhould neither have eyes, nor ears, nor tongues, therefore I am always blind, deaf and dumb, let me hear or fee what I may.

Wel. Lower your voice, you may be over- heard.

Hon. Then there is Sir Buzzard's filter, the widow, though her hufband is not dead fix months, is frifky and brifk----gadding about, and running mad for another——

Wel. Speak low, a gentleman lies ill in the next room.

Hon. As to Sir Buzzard, they have put their

fingers

fingers into his eyes fo often, he is blind as a beetle. I muſt make you laugh about the widow----

Wel. I cannot permit you to ſtay any longer from your Lady. Here's for your good report
(gives money.)

Hon. Dear Sir, you diſtreſs me---

Wel. Farewell---*(puſhing her out.)*
[*Exit* Honor.

Heav'n be prais'd ! I ·have got rid of you !--- Now to relieve my widow, who I ſuppoſe is mortified into humility, or burſting with rage.

Enter Widow *from the cloſet.*

Madam, I feel for your ſituation, and did every thing in my power to ſtop the impetuous flow of the woman's tongue-- but be not af- fected at what ſhe ſaid---" Cenſure and calum- ny are taxes paid by the moſt elevated charac- ters, nor is it poſſible to make defence againſt the impoſt, but by obſcurity."

Wid. It is beneath me, Sir, to defend my character againſt the aſperſions of ſo mean a wretch---I feel however for the impreſſions her falſhoods may have made on you.

Enter Muslin.

Muſ. You ſeem frightened, madam, quite fluſter'd I proteſt---ſure the gentleman attempted no rudeneſs---

Wid. That woman has ſlandered me groſly !

G 2   *Wel.*

Wel. Soothe your paſſion, madam, nothing ſo prejudicial to beauty as intemperate warmth ---conſider the vulgar ſet up a preſcription, for exerciſing latitude of tongue, that ſhews no reſpect to perſons.

Wid. Your hand, Mrs. Muſlin---ſome drops ---ſome water---I faint--- am overcome---I die! oh! *(faints in Welford's arms.)*

Muſ. Support her, dear Sir, 'till I return--- let me run for reſtoratives---- *(going, returns)* open her hands, chafe her temples,---a-lack a day---This is a maſter ſtroke of the widow's! *(aſide.)* [*Exit* Mus.

Wel. This is worſe than the ſtate of Tantalus---human nature cannot hold out---ſhe is really handſome. I will venture to kiſs her however---

Re-enter Muslin.

Muſ. Madam, Sir,---there is Miſs Conſtance and Colonel Staff with her---

Wid. What will become of me? *(Springing from the couch.)*

Wel. What will become of me?

Enter Colonel Staff.

Col. In his private chamber, and juſt ſprung from his arms!---Oh, hell and furies! but I will be cool,---we, Sir, will meet hereafter; this intruſion, madam, is, I ſee, as unſeaſonable as unexpected; I am ſorry to have interrupted you.

Wid.

Wid. I am unconcerned at your suspicions, Colonel,——you will not be censorious, Miss Constance---my business here was to prevent that imprudent step which you are about to take.

Con. You have succeeded, madam (*going*).

Wel. Will you hear me?

Con. I am forty, Sir, for the confusion I have caused---having gained my esteem without difficulty---you have resign'd it with the same ease—

Col. (*To the* Widow) This undeniable proof of your duplicity has reinstated my senses, and I will run the gauntlet no longer---you see I am calm---quite calm,---but I will have revenge ;--- you, Sir ?—

Wel. Well, Sir!---it is my duty to clear this lady from suspicion, to which her situation lays her open, and in which I am innocently involved.

Wid. You may have an interest in justifying yourself, Sir, but I request not to be included in your defence; I am going.

Col. I give up the pursuit——Madam, if my acts and deeds——

Wid. Your acts and deeds! Yes, I have heard of your acts and deeds from yourself, Colonel——but, be assured, a man without spirit shall never controul the acts and deeds of my fortune.

[*Exit.* Widow.

Col. A true Parthian,---she shot as she flew.

[*Exit.* Colonel.

Wel. Constance, will you attend to me?

Con. No, Sir,---you need not take the trouble
of

of fpeaking to me now, or of enquiring for me hereafter. [*Exit*. Conftance.

Wel. Was ever man fo unfortunate!---to have all my wifhes blafted in the moment of ripening!---to lofe the objeƈt of my love in the inftant of recovering her---who waits there? to have an intrigue with a wife, a widow, and a maid, in the courfe of one day, and be dif-appointed in all---will nobody anfwer? (*calling loud.*)

Enter M u s l i n.

Muf. What is the mater, Sir?
Wel. Where is the lady?
Muf. She went out with the Colonel.
Wel. I fpeak of the young lady.
Muf. She left the houfe in a chair,---but I cannot tell where fhe went.
Wel. I will this inftant to Sir Buzzard's!---I will follow her over the world;-- what an un-fortunate fellow!--- [*Exit*. Welford.

SCENE changes to the Parade. Enter CHEATERLY, *followed by a fervant.*

Cheat. What anfwer has Doƈtor Spruce fent?
Serv. He faid, Sir, he would not write,- -but remember your ungenerous treatment, and have revenge!---pardon me, Sir, but thefe were his words.
Cheat. Would have revenge?
Serv. Yes, Sir, and I faw a letter on his table direƈted to Sir Buzzard Savage;---there was an
attorney

attorney with him, and I heard him fay the penalty is treble the money loft.

Cheat. How much is he arrefted for ?

Serv. Upwards of feventy pounds.

Cheat. Here is a note for a hundred--- (*gives
a note*) fly and get him difcharged.

[*Exit* Servant.

A letter to Sir Buzzard !---an attorney with
him !---treble the penalty !---this Spruce I fear
will turn traitor.

Enter Douglas.

Captain Douglas, your moft obedient,-----
how long have you been in Bath ? I have not
feen you for an age.

Doug. I believe, Sir, not fince the York meeting, when my friend De Courcy loft his money.

Cheat. He is too ardent to attempt play,---
always off his guard.

Doug. And had the misfortune to play with
thofe who kept a conftant centinel upon his
weaknefs ;---he confided in you, and was de-
ceived ;---care, and a plain underftanding, may
preferve a man's property from the plunder of
a common robber,---but honefty' has no protection from the frauds of fuperior cunning.

Cheat. I won nothing from him ;---I loft----
the truth is, the knowing ones took us in.-----

Doug. But you fhared the winnings---

Cheat. Will you dare---

Doug. I will dare any thing that is honeft.

Cheat.

Cheat. Your friend, Sir, has dared to traduce my character, by the imputation you infinuate. But he and you fhould know me better, than to fuppofe any man could affront me with impuni·ty. (*lays his hand on his fword.*)

Doug. I know you have a mind capable of vindicating your conduct, even at the rifque of your own life, and the life of him you have in-jured---men like you, habituated in deceit, become callous to humanity;---deftitute of prin-ciple,---they are not deterred by the compunc-tions of confcience,---but will infure the profits of their cunning, even at the price of blood.

Cheat. My family, Sir---

Doug. Is honourable!---fpeak not of your family----their virtues render your vices the more confpicuous.

Enter Sir BUZZARD.

Sir Buz. Oh you traitor!---the reverend Mr. Spruce has made a full confeffion.----So I have been your pigeon, but the law fhall do me juftice.

Cheat. This is your fcheme, pufillanimous, mean wretch--- (*to Sir Buzzard*) for you, Sir, (*to Douglas*) we fhall meet again.

[*Exit* Cheaterly.

Sir Buz. Yes,---at the next affizes;---the fel-low's mind is fowed with hempfeed, and will yet produce a halter,---or if he efcapes hanging, I fhall fee him perifhing in a gaol, under as many wants as are in the Daily Advertifer;---have you been pigeon'd, Sir?

Doug.

Doug. No Sir.

Sir Buz. I have,---he has pluck'd fome quill feathers from me,---he has pinion'd me!---oh the rafcal!---but I fhall recover my mortgages, and bonds, with treble penalties!

Enter WELFORD *and Lady* FLIPPANT.

Wel. Diftraction!---fhe is loft!---I have been at your houfe, my Lady,---at Mr. Ordeal's---at every inn in the town,---but can get no tidings of her.

Lady Flip. It is furprifing, you, who poffefs a heart open and liberal, panting with affection for the whole fex, fhould run diftracted for the lofs of an individual!

Doug. You overlook me, Welford----

Wel. Douglas!---my friend!---O, Douglas, I have loft my Conftance!---I---

Lady Flip. No truant, I have been your ad-vocate and regained her for you---on condition of repentance---.

Enter CONSTANCE *and* CLARA *followed by* OR-DEAL.

Wel. My life!--- *(they embrace.)*

Sir Buz. Repentance!---let him marry, and he will live and die in a ftate of repentance.

Con. What!---marry me, an orphan without a fhilling?

Wel. Talk not of wealth,---were the riches of the world in your poffeffion, by Heaven they would not add a grain to the eftimation of your worth.

Ord. Generous and noble!

H

Con-

Con. (*to Ord.*) How, Sir, can I repay your generofity ?

Ord. The fatisfaction which refults from aiding virtue in diftrefs, is the only intereft a generous mind can wifh to receive for its fervices ;---becaufe it is the only intereft fuch a mind can enjoy.

Lady Flip. Return to my houfe ;---there you fhall be acquainted with a matter which nearly concerns your happinefs.

Sir Buz. Which I never expect to tafte !

Ord. Your happinefs is in your own power, commence the practice of virtue, and you will be enamoured of its fweets,--try the experiment, and never fear fuccefs.

Lady Flip. What fay you to that, Sir Buzzard ?

Sir Buz. I fay a man can never be too old to mend---I fay I have been pofitive all my life, and I fay if you follow the advice of your ancient and fapient friend, my endeavours to procure domeftic happinefs fhall not be wanting--- Ordeal, the laugh will be againft us both.

Ord. Laugh at me as long as you pleafe, but had I married Clara, the laugh would have been ftill ftronger againft me ;-----the Scot has done right, and the girl has done right, ---the mutual inclination of two virtuous fouls, cannot but render them more virtuous ;----the inhabitants of countries united by nature and policy fhould take every opportunity of ftrengthening the connexion ;---I fee you all think as I do !----and here I hope we fhall alfo meet approbation.

(*Bowing to the audience.*)

F I N I S.

EPILOGUE

To FASHIONABLE LEVITIES.

(As spoken by Miss YOUNGE.)

OUR growing Levities too clearly show,
  That all our troubles from refinement flow.
Two ages since we valu'd plain attire,
Blue-apron'd was the Dame, straight-hair'd the Squire;
They call'd not houshold bus'ness vulgar cares,
Nor deem'd it ungenteel to say their pray'rs:
But arts improv'd, new Levities arose,
And Ladies chang'd the fashion of their clothes;
Hoop'd petticoats in ev'ry town were seen:
The snug rotunda pleas'd the virgin Queen,
And beef for breakfast serv'd her Lady-train;
No wonder that her sailors baffled Spain.
Yet still we've chiefs with love of glory fir'd;
But so had Rome when liberty expired;
" We've statesmen too, who burn with patriots flame,
" But so had Greece, when Greece had lost her fame."
" We've admirals who plow the briny deep,
" Through azure skies and rolling clouds they sweep,
" Invade the Planets in an Air Balloon,
" And fright from her propriety the Moon"—
Bess was a man, when danger call'd her pow'rs,
She was a woman in her private hours—
Few Levities, few luxuries she knew;
No cherries then in February grew:
May-dukes in April on the bough hung green,
And girls wore hanging-sleeves till full eighteen.
Few mothers teach their daughters grace or sense;
But tell them taste in dress is excellence:
Bid them the Levities of rank assume,
And flaunt with spreading bow, or nodding plume;

                           Strut

Strut in a riding-drefs, to fhew their fhapes;
Or ftalk in boots, and coats with tripple capes.
Affecting eafe, but impudently free,
The matron leans upon her cicifbee;
While *cara fpofa* fnugly keeps his wench,'
Defies his duns, and revels in the Bench.
" Why, this is vice, not folly?" I agree;
But ftill this vice proceeds from Levity.
Some fouls there are which moral fenfe fublimes,
A few bleft fpirits in the worft of times;
One in whom birth and piety are join'd;
Of native worth, and truly royal mind;
Who with benignant hand her bleffings pours;
Who knows no Levities, but feels for yours,

⁎ *Thofe lines which are not marked with inverted commas,
were taken from an epilogue written by Mr. Norris, for the author of the comedy.*